Dedalus Europe
General Editor: Timothy L

The Tower
at the
Edge of the World

William Heinesen

The Tower
at the
Edge of the World

Translated by W. Glyn Jones

Dedalus

Dedalus would like to thank the Danish Arts Foundation and Arts Council, England for their assistance in producing this book.

DANISH ARTS FOUNDATION

Published in the UK by Dedalus Limited
24-26, St Judith's Lane, Sawtry, Cambs, PE28 5XE
email: info@dedalusbooks.com
www.dedalusbooks.com

ISBN printed book 978 1 910213 66 7
ISBN ebook 978 1 910213 73 5

Dedalus is distributed in the USA & Canada by SCB Distributors
15608 South New Century Drive, Gardena, CA 90248
email: info@scbdistributors.com   web: www.scbdistributors.com

Dedalus is distributed in Australia by Peribo Pty Ltd
58, Beaumont Road, Mount Kuring-gai, N.S.W. 2080
email: info@peribo.com.au

Publishing History
First published in Denmark as *Tarnet ved verdens ende* in 1976
First Published by Dedalus in 2018

Printed and bound in Great Britain by Clays Ltd, St Ives plc
Typeset by Marie Lane

The Author

William Heinesen (1900–1991) was born in Torshavn in the Faroe Islands, the son of a Danish mother and Faroese father, and was equally at home in both languages. Although he spent most of his life in the Faroe Islands he chose to write in Danish as he felt it offered him greater inventive freedom. Although internationally known as a poet and a novelist he made his living as an artist. His paintings range from large-scale murals in public buildings, through oil to pen sketches, caricatures and collages.

It is Dedalus' intention to make all of William Heinesen's novels available in new translations by W. Glyn Jones. Published so far are: *The Black Cauldron*, *The Lost Musicians*, *Windswept Dawn*, *The Good Hope*, *Mother Pleiades* and *The Tower at the Edge of the World*, to be followed in 2019 by *Noatun*.

William Heinesen is generally considered to be one of the greatest, if not the greatest, Scandinavian novelist of the twentieth century.

The Translator

W. Glyn Jones (1928–2014) had a distinguished career as an academic, a writer and a translator.

He taught at various universities in England and Scandinavia before becoming Professor of Scandinavian Studies at Newcastle and then at the University of East Anglia. He also spent two years as Professor of Scandinavian Literature in the Faroese Academy. On his retirement from teaching he was created a Knight of the Royal Danish Order of the Dannebrog. He has written widely on Danish, Faroese and Finland-Swedish literature including studies of Johannes Jorgensen, Tove Jansson and William Heinesen. He is the author of *Denmark: A Modern History* and co-author with his wife, Kirsten Gade, of *Colloquial Danish* and the *Blue Guide to Denmark*.

W. Glyn Jones' many translations from Danish include *Seneca* by Villy Sorensen and for Dedalus: *The Black Cauldron, The Lost Musicians, Windswept Dawn, The Good Hope, Mother Pleiades* and *The Tower at the Edge of the World* by William Heinesen, *Ida Brandt* and *As Trains Pass By (Katinka)* by Herman Bang and *My Fairy-Tale Life* by Hans Christian Andersen.

Before he died, Glyn translated William Heinesen's novel *Nòatun* which Dedalus will publish in 2019.

The Tower at the Edge of the World

A poetic mosaic novel about
earliest childhood

See, my friends; the grass turns green.
The cold bites, the wind blows,
The snow swirls,
But the grass turns green,
And deep, deep is my green happiness.

See, my friends: the grass turns green.
Tired is my foot, hairless my head,
Toothless my mouth, dimmed my eye.
Soon I shall leave you,
But my heart flowers
And deep, deep
Is my green happiness today.

Li Po

In the Days when the Earth was not yet Round but had a Beginning and an End,

a splendid tower could be seen at the furthermost
edge of the world.

During the daytime an endless procession of clouds floated slowly past out there in the void under the eye of the sun.

At night, the tower shone out and competed with the Northern Lights and the stars over the void, for it was a tower of light.

On clear evenings you could see the tower's beautiful light shining out in the darkness over the sea, and then you could be caught by an irresistible urge to reach this shining tower rising in isolation out there towards the vast unknown areas where the world ends and begins and the Spirit of God hovers over the waters.

It was in the far-off time of beginnings, when you still didn't know that the magical light from the tower was the light from a quite ordinary lighthouse, a work of human hands and ingenuity, a useful and sensible provider of light whose task it is to be a guide for those sailing the seas.

And it was also before you yet knew that the Earth is a star among other stars in an inconceivable gulf of time and Space, and that you yourself are a star dweller.

11

The Evening Horn

Yes, the Earth with its lighthouses and ships, islands and lands, cities and peoples, is a star, one of the many beautiful radiant heavenly bodies in the firmament.

But *you* don't know that yet, for you are quite new to the world of words and for the time being you must cope with sounds and images as best you can.

You are at the restless but delicious focal point of your beginning. It's early spring, and you are lying in your bed, new in time, unknowing, but filled with immense intimations.

There you lie, listening to the Evening Horn.

The Evening Horn, that's the sound made by the golden stripe in the sky, over there where the sun sank into the sea.

It's a big, happy bird cackling and clucking.

It's the Evening Bird.

No, it's the Ferryman sitting out there on the rocks outside his house, blowing his horn.

The Evening Bird clucks and cackles in the Ferryman's horn. The yellow line in the sky is his horn. There's a quiet lapping sound of happily rocking waters in his horn.

Then twilight comes. Then darkness comes. Then the horn falls silent.

The Tap

Then night comes.

Night rests on all roofs.

Night twinkles in all windows and in the pools of rain on the lids of the blue paraffin drums.

Now everyone is slumbering in their bedrooms, where

sleep flowers float down in the darkness.

The distant sound of star drops falling from the heavens can be heard in the silence. The sound echoes throughout the vast vault of heaven.

The sound is the only sound in Heaven and on Earth.

It's only the sound of a tap that hasn't been turned off properly.

The dripping tap is alone, alone in the world.

Smoke

There are no beams spanning the heavenly loft.

There is an empty bed in the garden outside the Old Man's house. It is made of wood and has recently been scrubbed. It is to stand there and dry in the sunshine, but there *is* no real sunshine, for the Old Man is sitting on the edge of his bed smoking his pipe, and in the huge cloud of smoke the sun turns red and dull.

The Old Man sits looking up at the heavenly loft, where the smoke gathers in great clouds.

Finally, there is no cloud to be seen either, just smoke and mist.

***

Both the bed and the Old Man are gone in the evening, and the sun is shining beautifully on the Old Man's roof now.

The Words

The words come flying in. Or they drift down quite gently. Or they fix themselves on the windowpane in the shape of raindrops or ice flowers.

The words stand there like flower bulbs in vases, covered by grey paper cones. Then one day the cones are gone, and that means the sweet-smelling hyacinths and tulips are on their way.

Hyacinth and tulip are the loveliest of words. You never tire of saying them and playing with them. "Tulip and hyacinth, hyalip and tulicinth – citilip – hyatul – tulihy."

God's Floor

The world is vast.

It is made up partly of land and partly of water, but mostly of water. Wherever you turn your eyes, you can see water twinkling somewhere or other and you can hear the sound it makes, and sometimes you can even stand there and see God floating over the waters like a shining cloud.

But there is a lot of land too, with mountains and valleys.

Far towards the north there is the heath with its heather-covered hills and busy babbling brooks, some of them babbling in the darkness under the ground. Even further away to the north, where the sun sets in the summer, stand the Faraway Mountains. The highest of the Faraway Mountains has a flat top. That is God's floor. That is where He rests when He's tired of floating over the waters out in the abyss.

God's Floor is set with grey tablets of stone that are swept and scrubbed clean by the wind and the rain. Somewhere among the stones there is a big grey expanse of moss filled with little pink flowers. That is God's pillow.

God's tablets are full of writing.

God stands on his stone floor and looks out over the world during the white nights. "His eye seeth every precious thing".

Then he kneels down and fills the big tablets with writing.

The Summer Girls

There is no night during the summer. So it's always light, and the world is filled with Summer Girls.

You can hear them laughing and singing everywhere – in living rooms and kitchens, on stairs and in doorways, in the wind down by the shore and out on the billowing fields.

They are always there with their hair and their clothes and hands that smell of pencil or salami or of tansy and cress. The summer girls sit swinging their big legs on swaying branches. They walk on stilts. They play hide and seek among fences and outbuildings. They sit on the edges of ditches and thread flowers on strings. They look at picture books. They make little fans of pictures on the walls above their beds.

They sit and sing by your bed in the evening.

One of them comes to you only when you are asleep. Suddenly, she is *there*, staring at you with big eyes. She doesn't speak; she doesn't touch you; she simply stares.

You have to go with her, floating low over the earth, through streets that are deserted at night, across stretches of heather and gently whispering waters and into the pale heavens far away at the End of the World, where the Tower stands.

Time Flies

Fly is a lovely word. The wind flies past, the clouds fly past, the waves fly out on the water.

Time flies.

"Why does time fly?"

"Because it's in a hurry."

"Why is it in a hurry?"

"Because there's so much it has to do."
"Where does it hurry to?"
Silence.
"What is time?"
Long silence.
"Is it everything that flies?"
"Yes, that's it. It's everything that flies."

The Earth Girl Lonela

The Earth isn't round yet and God has still not established a borderline between dreaming and waking or between fleeting shadows and living persons.

Down in the coal cellar's everlasting night sits the Earth Girl Lonela. She is only to be seen for a brief moment just as we go down with the torch to fetch coal. There she is, sitting in the corner, and behind her there is a host of grey faces and hands. These are all the other earth girls who live down here.

Then they all vanish, and where the Earth Girl Lonela was there is nothing to be seen but the shadow of an old notched piece of driftwood.

But then for a moment you have seen how she sits staring at you, for she knows you well.

***

The Earth Girl Lonela and all the other earth girls live in the dark beneath the house and they never see the light of day, for they are *dead*.

The Earth Girl Lonela has big night eyes. She sits there longing to go up into the daylight, but she has to stay down in the dark.

Who is the Earth Girl Lonela?

Perhaps a girl who once lived in the house long ago. But then one evening she was gone. Her parents searched high and low for her, going around lighting up the darkness with torches and lamps, but all they could see was the old tree root and its shadow. Lonela could see her parents all right. But she had to stay where she was, for she was dead.

***

On Judgement Day, when the trumpet sounds, the whole house will collapse with a great din, and the cherubs will come with their flaming swords and split the old tree root.

Then the dead will come back to life. Then Lonela and all the other pale earth girls will come milling up out of the ground and float into the light and the day.

But the Earth Girl Lonela isn't so dead that during the night she can't creep up out of the coal cellar into the hallway and further up the stairs into the loft and the bedroom where you lie dreaming. Then you know that she has come to fetch you and that the two of you are going out to *float*. Out to float on great wings, over sea and over land, all the way to the End of the World, where the Tower stands.

Debes, the Lighthouse Keeper

The Tower at the End of the World isn't the only tower in the world, for the world is full of towers. The "Tower of Babel". The "Leaning Tower of Pisa". The "Round Tower" in Copenhagen. The "Eiffel Tower" in Paris.

But the Tower at the End of the World is the highest and strangest of all towers. There it stands on the edge of the great abyss shining out in the darkness, and so huge is it that it takes a whole day to get up to the shining eye at the top.

Debes, the Lighthouse Keeper is to be found up there.

"Debes, the Lighthouse Keeper – is he a spirit? Or is he a cherub?"

"Don't talk silly. Debes the Lighthouse Keeper is a perfectly ordinary man."

"But why does he stay up in the tower?"

"He stays up there to make sure the light doesn't go out."

Debes the Lighthouse Keeper sits staring out into the darkness and listening to the great rushing sound from the abyss. Sometimes, the light from the tower catches a big cloud coming floating slowly over the abyss, and when it gets closer, the lighthouse keeper can see that it has a huge face and dreadful eyes. That's God floating by on His endless travels. Then the lighthouse keeper has to hide his eyes in his hands and sit and wait until the cloud has floated past. He peeps out through his fingers to see whether it's still there – ugh yes, it's still there giving him threatening looks.

So it's a good job he hasn't been asleep. For sometimes the lighthouse keeper is so tired from having to stay awake all night that he can't keep his eyes open. But then he is awakened by a deafening voice:

"Debes! *Are you asleep*?"

"Oh no. Oh no."

"Yes you were. You were asleep. Why do you lie to me, the Lord your God?"

Then the lighthouse keeper has to admit that he had been asleep, for it's no use lying to God, who sees everything.

And God shakes His great cloud head, and His voice re-echoes in the abyss, full of anguish.

"I thought I could rely on you, Debes the Lighthouse Keeper."

18

Then the lighthouse keeper weeps the bitter tears of repentance, while the solitary cloud floats away and disappears in the void.

The Sledge Ride

Oh, winter has come. It's snowing and snowing.

After a brilliant day with games in the snow: now it is evening, green and alluring over darkening fells.

Just one more last sledge ride down the hill and out into the desolate evening space!

Alone in the world. Alone with the snow's pure scent of nothing! All the daytime children have gone, but tiny white Night Children are dancing in the dusk, dancing in the drifting snow, dancing joyfully and ecstatically up and down the evening's green icy steps.

But the deep snowdrift where the sledge usually stops of its own accord – that snowdrift has gone now, and now there's a new slope, such a long, long one. And then comes a big flat surface with lots of shining stars above, and the sledge glides on of its own accord, although there is no hill here – on and on until there is nothing but air and stars, and now your sledge is floating through nothing at all. And far away – oh, just look – far away there is a tower rising towards the heavens, and that is the Tower at the End of the World. The top is shining and sparkling like a sparkler; it looks so cheerful that you have to laugh aloud; but only for a moment, for suddenly you realise that you are alone and so far away that you will never be able to find your way home again.

Then you wake up with a cry in your bed.

"What's wrong, Amaldus? Have you had a bad dream?"

"Yes, I dreamt I was at the End of the World, the place where that Tower is."

New Year

It's New Year. So everything is new.

All the streams and lakes are covered with ice – so where are you going to sail, my little ship, my Christmas present?

Oh well, then it'll have to wait.

And then you'll all have to wait, captain and mate, boatswain and apprentice and cook and cook's mate (oh, all these lovely words!) while the snow snows and the frost freezes.

***

Then, on the very first day of the New Year, the thaw set in; the snow melted and the ice broke up, and the little green schooner the *Christina*, the one with the bluish white sails, could be seen rocking there in a quiet cove beneath a flame-gold afternoon sky with great clouds and a lovely scent of earth and water.

It was New Year, and like your new ship, everything was new. And the New Moon hung low in the sky.

It's Late in the Year and Late in the Day and Late in Life.

The dusk is turning into darkness and the first stars can be seen. It looks like being a clear starry night.

Before me on the table where I (Amaldus the Reminiscer, the Ageing One) am sitting to write, lies Father's old telescopic Nelson spyglass with the highly polished brass fittings; it's still in good condition, and I intend shortly to go out beneath the sky to turn it towards the Andromeda Galaxy, that distant universe that is supposed to be two million light years away – not something to be scoffed at when you consider that a light year is the distance light travels in a year at a speed of 300,000 kilometres a second. It gives you a delightful sense of elbowroom to stand and gaze down into this vast past, even if what you see is only a faint, dying smoking flax in the night.

"Like the light from a horn lamp," said the ancient Chaldeans of the light from this world behind the world, and the image remains with you, for a dark, cloudy lamp such as this was what we used to light our way long ago in our faraway childhood through murky alleyways between houses that no longer exist. It was admittedly no horn lamp, but an empty tin with greaseproof paper tied over the open end and with a stump of candle inside and a hole in the "roof" through which the candle could breathe.

And so we went with this Andromeda mist and *shone a light*, somewhere far away in time, which in those days still had the dimensions of eternity.

***

Who is it lighting the way with the old veiled world lamp deep down there at the bottom of time?

A little boy and a young woman, and the young woman is his mother. They walk in the quiet evening through winding alleyways bathed in an emanation of seaweed and peat smoke, and they proceed further through hay-scented paths out to the Redoubt. There they sit and watch the darkness growing and becoming all powerful. When he holds the lamp up in front of his mother's face it shines like a moon on her cheeks and mouth and chin. Then this face is all that is to be seen – nothing else in the whole world but this face standing out tenderly against the vast darkness.

Then for a moment it can be anywhere at all at any time, and you are without name or history, you are simply Mother and Child, the first and the last.

Music from the Sea

That curious little machine with the grey roll that turns round and round and the big green horn is called the Phonograph. It belongs to Uncle Christoffer, who is a sailor and sails in foreign ships out on the great oceans. He has come home on a visit now.

Frail, hoarse but charming music issues from the phonograph horn, music that reminds you of the rushing sound that comes from a shell or the gentle shushing sound of sea and shore in calm weather.

Your mother and your aunts know this music well and they tell you what it is called: "Annie Laurie", "Zampa", "Les millions d'Harlequin" (lovely words, the sound of which will never be forgotten).

***

When Uncle Christoffer went to sea again, he left his miracle machine behind. The frail wax rollers were gradually worn out, and the music became ever more distant and muffled week by week until it was finally lost in an almost tuneless soughing, a final sigh of wind and wave, as though it had once more been swallowed up by the vast, remote distance from which it came.

William Heinesen

Deaf Jane

The Earth Girl Lonela is no longer a living person like you yourself and your parents and Aunt Nanna are. The Earth Girl Lonela can't speak or smile, but only stare. She only exists in dreams.

It's rather different, though not very different, with Deaf Jane. She can't speak either. But she can still smile.

Deaf Jane always comes in the evening. She is terribly pale. She picks politely at her food. She smells of paraffin and lambskin.

Deaf Jane lives alone. She sews for people. There is a rancid smell of grease about her sewing machine. All her little living room in Bakkehellen smells of grease and lamb and paraffin.

There is a parti-coloured patchwork quilt on her bed in the corner and in front of the bed a white lambskin rug. On the windowsill there is a plant pot full of flowers with velvet leaves, yellow and dark blue; they are called "pansies".

Deaf Jane has a paraffin heater and a paraffin stove. Her fingers are thin and clammy. Her eyes glare.

"No, they don't *glare*. Jane has lovely eyes."

"Lovely eyes." So that's what lovely eyes look like. They are velvet and soft like pansies. Warm, damp, clammy.

The tightly curled lambskin by Jane's bed is the skin from a poor dead baby lamb.

When Jane has settled down in the evening, she lies there with her hands folded and stares with clammy but lovely eyes up at the ceiling while she says her prayers:

> Father, upon this bed of mine,
> Cast those loving eyes divine.

***

One evening, as Jane was in the hall putting on her coat, you went across and touched her. Just gently touched her hand to feel if she really was a living person.

And then she smiled at you with her lovely eyes and bent down and quickly put her mouth against your hair.

Stare-Eyes

The church smells of old cupboards and drawers, of shoe polish and leather hymn books. People sit within the confines of their box pews. When they sing you can see the *spirit* flowing from their mouths like mist.

In the flickering light from two big candles: the altarpiece in which the sexton and the parish clerk are lowering the minister's dead body with its dreadfully thin arms and legs down into the grave.

But the same minister is also standing in the pulpit. He is pale and thin and has a thin red beard and strangely sorrowful eyes like a hungry bird begging for crumbs.

The big ship hanging under the roof slowly turns around on its cord, sometimes showing the big window in the stern and sometimes the dark gun ports. It is sailing through time. It sails and sails, and yet it always stays where it is.

In the grey Sunday weather outdoors, the winds rushes through the withered grass on the house roofs, and the ships at anchor out in the cove pitch and toss as though in endless sorrow and sail and sail without going anywhere.

The entire church is also a ship sailing. On the bench at the back there sit stooping seamen with melancholy bearded faces

24

and big helpless hands full of sores and scratches. They are the church's crew. In drawling voices they sing:

Oh, living God, guide our ship to port.

***

Stare-Eyes sits in one of the pews. That is the name you give her because she sits and stares. She always sits in the same pew, between her parents and her sisters. She stares at you, and so you have to stare back at her.

Stare-Eyes sings so loud and clear that you can easily distinguish her voice from the others. Stare-Eyes' hair is very long and gathered in two heavy plaits, brown tied with blue bows. She has a small nose, but big, staring eyes. She stares at you like the Earth Girl Lonela when she comes to your bed in the evenings to take you out floating with her.

You didn't like the way Stare-Eyes looked at you and you turned your eyes in a different direction, but even so, you couldn't refrain from peeping at her pew to see whether those staring eyes were still there.

Yes, they are still there, and now you also have a feeling that she is laughing as though she knows something about you or as if she knows what you are thinking about as you sit there.

But one Sunday, Stare-Eyes was not at church, and then you missed her eyes after all.

If –

So much can *happen* in the world. Dreadful things can happen. That knowledge makes you think sad thoughts.

Your mother can *die*. That is the most dreadful thing of all.

First you fall ill. Then you die.

Mother is ill. She lies there, quite pale and far away. Two women sit by her bed. They sit and *wait*. One of them is knitting. The other is doing something or other with warm water and linen.

Mother reaches out a clammy hand to you. She smiles, but her eyes are strangely far away. There is a vase of dark red flowers on the chest of drawers. They are roses. They smell sweet and sharp so it catches your nose and makes your eyes smart. There are thorns like cat's claws on the stems.

"Come on, Amaldus. We'll go out and buy some *lucky dips*."

Aunt Nanna is dressed for winter, in long buttoned boots and with a fur-edged jersey and mittens. She is *radiant*. You've heard someone say that she is radiant. It sounds funny. It is otherwise only light that is radiant. No, red roses can be radiant as well...

The lucky dips are pale blue. There's a shiny picture on each packet. There are "peppermints" in the packets, and then a *thing*: perhaps a ring for your finger, perhaps a hat made of lovely crumpled tissue paper, perhaps a piece of black liquorice or a little whistle.

The ring cuts into your finger, the shrill sound of the whistle hurts your ears, and the peppermint taste burns your tongue. You don't like the blue lucky dips with their rings and whistles. You want to cry at the thought of the red roses and their nasty cat's claws, and of the silent women and your sick mother.

When you die, you are put in the ground and lie there all on your own in the cemetery.

"But your soul goes up to God in Heaven."

But that's a very long way away, high up beyond the highest of those mountains in the distance, or far out beyond the End

26

of the World.

The wind is blowing in from the grey sea. It blows into your mouth and your nose so that you are blown right away in all that wind.

At last there is nothing but this cruel wind, filled with the harsh cries of birds and the flapping of half dry clothes on a clothes line.

And then there's a song, the saddest of all, although Aunt Nanna is *radiant* as she sings it:

> And fare thee well, my only love,
> And fare thee well a while!
> And I will come again, my love,
> Tho' it were ten thousand miles!

For then you have to think of the red roses and their over-powering perfume and their bent cat's claws.

And that terrible word *if* –

***

You didn't sleep at home that night, but in Grandmother's house, *Andreasminde*, in a deep alcove bed where Aunt Nanna slept along with her two sisters Kaja and Mona. It was a tight squeeze, and you got an elbow in your eye, but that was not why you wept and couldn't fall asleep. It was the fault of those dreadful roses: you couldn't get them out of your mind, and neither could you get away from Aunt Nanna's sweet melody, "Fare thee well..."

When you woke the following morning, you were alone in bed, but soon afterwards Aunt Nanna came in, and she was radiant.

"Amaldus, my dear, you're not an *only* child any longer, for you've got a little brother."

Later on, you went home and saw this little brother, but only the back of his neck, for he lay there with a down-covered head burrowed deep in Mother's breast.

The red roses were still there, but they looked all down in the dumps, for they had been given the company of some pale blue hyacinths that quite overpowered them with their perfume.

Sailing at Dawn

What else happened during this strange time before the Earth grew round?

Lots of things, lots of things. For in that great gulf extending from God's Floor in the north to the Furthermost Edge far to the south, the days are still like months and the months like years. But the world, which in the beginning was only a place where a helpless, crying refugee from nothingness sought a simple shelter, has long been a splendid playground full of exciting things, full of light and air, music and new magical words...

Sun and Moon take it in turns to show themselves in the sky; the wind hurries by and the rain rains, the sea grows dark and then grows light; ships weigh anchor and set sail and become fading shadows and nothing at all out in the immeasurable waste, but the shadows come back and turn into ships again.

One of these ships is the *Christina*, of which Father is captain. The *Christina* is a big schooner that is almost always at sea for it sails to Leith and Copenhagen and brings goods home to the Rømer Concern.

You've already often been on board the *Christina*, but only when the ship was at anchor in the roads. But then one morning it happened that the *Christina* had an errand in a harbour on another island and you were allowed to sail on it. It was an early morning with lighthouses lit and lots of twinkling stars.

And there you are now, standing on the rocking deck in biting cold, listening to the mainsail ferociously rumbling and thundering before giving in to the wind and unfolding in peace and a vast sense of cheerfulness.

And now this morning ship is on its way – the creaking and groaning schooner with its masts and booms and ropes and with its bowsprit and tiller and windlass, its deckhouse and its pantry. All these new words with their cheerful names! And all of it in a pervasive scent of tar and bilge water, of fish and salt and smoke from the galley.

And this is the *sea*, blackish blue and green and whitish, with the thousands of whispering and murmuring mouths of the waves.

And the dark border out there in the far distance is the Horizon. The *Horizon!* The strangest of all words, so filled with terror and delight, for that is where the world ends; here is the Abyss, the vast bed where the Sun sleeps at night and the Moon and the Stars during the day. And that is where the Tower stands...

Yes, just look: there it is, right out on the Horizon, with a twinkling star at its top.

Now the *Christina's* grey sails turn blood red all at once, for now the Sun is on its way up from its depths. And suddenly it is revealed in the east, enormously big and flaming red in the morning haze. But it doesn't stand still; it rocks up and down like an enormous buoy, disappears behind vast ridges of breakers and emerges again, each time bigger and bigger and nearer to bursting and looking foreboding. And you are cold and your teeth are chattering, not only from cold, but also from fear; for see, the red pod around the Sun bursts, and its clear, dazzling fire bursts out and sets the sea ablaze!

But Father, at the wheel, yawns loudly and heartily and shows his big teeth in his beard, and so everything is after all probably as it should be, and the time for the End of the World and Judgement Day hasn't come yet.

No, for now the Sun turns grey and disappears in a darkening hail shower. The hailstones drum deafeningly against the distended sails and dance merrily on the deck. And when the Sun finally shows itself again, it has turned into an ordinary yellow everyday sun. It is day and normality; the world has become itself again, and the ship sails into a fjord and docks.

The Green Storehouse

Of all the remarkable houses in the town, the Green Storehouse is the most remarkable.

The Green Storehouse is a tall warehouse with low-ceilinged rooms and lots of steps. It smells everywhere of tar and ropes, of varnish and tobacco and spit from chewing tobacco.

In one of the rooms there is a little cubicle full of glass splinters. This is the Glass Room. Here stands the Window Man, cutting glass with a diamond that he has hanging in a string around his neck so that no one can come and steal it from him, for a diamond is the most precious thing in the world.

The Window Man is a pale, serious man with red eyes and a red nose.

The Window Man has had a sad fate.

"What's a sad fate?"

"It's when you've lost all you love."

"Has the Window Man lost his diamond?"

"No, but he's lost five of his six children; they all died of *consumption*. And the Window Man's wife died of consumption. Little Angelica's all he's got left now."

"Sad fate."

When the Window Man has scratched the glass with his diamond and carefully breaks off a piece to make a window pane, the glass says *"sad"*.

***

Ole Morske hangs out here in the Storehouse. He sits in a huge room right up at the top under the big skylight. That's the Sail Loft. He sits there with the edging of a sail over his knees like a huge duvet. He is a sailmaker. He doesn't answer when you ask him about anything, and so no one talks to him. But then he talks to himself and says strange things.

"She touched me to do me harm."

"They've killed a lot in that way."

Ole Morske builds small ships. He has several lovely ships standing on a shelf, schooners and sloops, fully rigged and shining with varnish and paint. Anton, the warehouse clerk, takes you up into the Sail Loft one day and shows you these fine ships. Ole Morske sits sewing a sail; all you see is the back of his woollen jersey and the old crumpled cloth hat he always wears.

In a corner of the big room stands *Rydberg's Horn*. *Rydberg's Horn* is a fog horn; it has a green horn and a handle, and when the handle is turned it makes a sound that is so terrible that you can go *mad* from hearing it.

"Is it *Rydberg's Horn* that made Ole Morske *mad?*"

"Ole Morske's not mad; he's just odd. He became odd when his wife ran away from him. He was quite out of his mind for a time then."

"What's mind?"

"It's what you think with."

"Did Ole Morske think a lot about his wife?"

Aunt Nanna purses her lips and blows in your face: *"Yes."*

One day, Anton came with two little ships, presents for you from Ole Morske. You were so incredibly happy at this and insisted on going up into the Sail Loft to thank him. He said nothing, and neither did he look at you, but his stubbly face was one big smile.

***

The Window Man often goes to the churchyard and potters around his six graves. Angelica goes with him and wanders around collecting mother-of-pearl from the crushed shells between the graves.

But early one morning, all the lowest panes of the church windows have been smashed, and the Window Man sits on the church doorstep with bleeding hands, swinging the diamond backwards and forwards like a pendulum.

"Poor man. Now little Angelica's dead as well, and he's gone completely out of his mind."

"Sad fate, sad fate."

(The Window Man got his mind back, but he's not the Window Man any longer, just an ordinary joiner, for he can't stand the sight of glass.)

***

That was the Glass Room and the Sail Loft. Then there's the Compass Room in the deep Storehouse cellar. This is where the *Ship Men* sit around a little table, drinking beer from blue tankards. They sit and laugh and thump the table and sometimes they quarrel and fight. But sometimes they sing and are happy.

The Ship Men are father's men, and you know them well. They sharpen your pencil, which is red at one end and blue at the other, and one of them can draw bearded faces with pipes in their mouths.

Sometimes there are also strangers sitting around the table in the compass room. One day, they are *Frenchmen*; they have black beards and the whites of their eyes are very white. Some of them are wearing flat red bonnets, and some have silver crosses in chains around their necks.

The Frenchmen have caught a dead man in their net, a corpse. No one knows who the dead man is.

The corpse has been put in the church and is to be buried. It's very sad, but the Frenchmen aren't sad; they are merry and make a din and sing about how they were enjoying themselves. They are happy because it's not them who are dead and turned into corpses.

The corpse was buried the next day, but by then the Frenchmen had gone. But nevertheless a lot of people accompanied the dead stranger to the grave, and Mother was one of them.

"For it could have been any of us. It could have been your father."

***

That was the Compass Room. Then there is the Bedroom.

The Bedroom is a small wallpapered room high up in the

southern end of the Storehouse. There is nothing here except a dusty table and an old blackened mirror on the wall above the table.

"Who sleeps here?"

"Nobody."

When you look at yourself in the black mirror, you don't see yourself: all you see is a grey shadow. That is Nobody.

Nobody sits on the empty table. Nobody stands at the gable window and looks out across the bay with its boats and ships and out across the sea and the horizon.

Behind the horizon lies the Big World, which Nobody can see. That's where the Eiffel Tower is and the Leaning Tower of Pisa, and further away there are the Egyptian Pyramids and the Tower of Babel, and furthest away of all, the Tower at the End of the World.

During the night, the half moon drifts slowly across the heavens like a capsized boat with no crew.

That's when Nobody opens the window and stands and stretches. He stretches his long arms out like wings and floats out into the night and looks in through all the bedroom windows, and if you are lying there awake and outside the window can see a face with big sad eyes, that is Nobody.

That's when Nobody smiles at you for a moment, lonely and poor, before he floats further off across the world with its towers and spires and further on through the cold rooms beneath the stars by the Furthermost Edge.

Afterwards, he comes back to his bedroom with its faded and discoloured wallpaper. Here he sits on the table beneath the black mirror, huddled up, with long arms round his bent knees.

Fortune

Then there was the Coffee House!

The Coffee House is a cosy little tarred building with a turf roof and small windows and a sooty chimney from which a great deal of smoke emerges.

Inside the Coffee House stands the big oven in which the coffee beans are roasted and the mill in which the roasted coffee beans are ground. This is where one-armed Coffee Pouline and her blind sister Anna work for the Rømer Concern, and here there is also almost always a third sister, Juliane the Sexton's wife, to be found. She sits on the bench near the low window, slumped between her two crutches, for she is paralysed and can't support herself on her legs. But the tiny bright eyes in her rough, as it were coffee-roasted face are full of laughter, as though she were sitting there thoroughly savouring all the funny things that happen in the world.

Juliane the Sexton's wife has also had a sad fate: her husband, Julius the Sexton was taken by the surf and drowned one stormy evening out near the White Sands Cove, where he had gone to rescue some driftwood, and that same year Juliane herself fell down from a stack of fish drying out on the Ring and broke both her thighs.

But Juliana nevertheless retained her good humour, which is fortunate for her and a blessing.

And Coffee Pouline and Blind Anna are also full of good humour, and they chat away while the beans are roasting in their drum and the flywheel in the coffee mill flies. Anna's eyes don't look blind at all, and she almost always laughs and smiles as though she is looking forward to something that is coming to her.

Now and then, the three sisters are visited by Spanish Rikke, who always has so much to tell them about what is going on in town. Then the coffee pan is put on the hob, and Pouline fetches four flower-decorated bowls from the wall cupboard, or five if Jacob the Baker happens to come in from the store bakery to have a snack. Jacob the Baker usually has a big, greasy paper bag with him that is full of cut-offs from Danish pastries and sugar buns.

Aunt Nanna, too, is often in the Coffee House. She sometimes comes to have her fortune told. Coffee Pouline is a fortune teller and can read the coffee grounds. Then everything goes quiet and there is a slightly uncomfortable feeling in the Coffee House while Pouline examines the bowl, and then Aunt Nanna sits there radiant and shivering and with her eyes closed for as long as it takes.

"If it's anything nasty, Pouline, you mustn't tell me, you know."

"Nasty and nasty – you never know, Nanna, but one thing I can tell you and that is that you'll have a suitor before this winter's out, and he is well dressed and wears a hat and a watch chain and all that, and he has a flower in his buttonhole and... what on earth is *that*? A pistol? No, nonsense, it's just a big cigar in a very fine cigar holder!"

Then Pouline pushes the bowl away and gives Aunt Nanna a tap on her bottom.

"And then the rest is up to you!"

Juliane the Sexton's wife: "Big cigar in a cigar holder! Did you hear that, Anna?"

Blind Anna (delightedly): "Yes, and a flower in his buttonhole."

***

Above the entrance to the Coffee House there is an old, worn horseshoe. Coffee Pouline herself found it and persuaded the Storehouse Keeper Anton to nail it on to the door frame.

"Yes, but why does it have to be there?"

Aunt Nanna (still a little radiant): "Because it means *good fortune*."

The Wise Virgins

Out on the coast along the bay, there is a row of black huts, all with their gables out towards the water, and in the evenings the sleepy light from the small windows in the gables is reflected and reproduced in countless shapes in the dark waters, twisting and twirling like eels.

The Wise Virgins live behind one of these gable windows.

They sit beneath their lighted wall lamp in the spotless kitchen, where the kettle sings on the stove and the cat lies in a straw basket with its kittens.

They sit reading the Holy Scriptures. They read about the End of the World and the Last Day that is soon to come. No one knows when, for it comes "like a thief in the night".

The Wise Virgins are poor and have nothing to live on except charitable gifts from good people, for they don't work for their food, but simply sit reading the Scriptures. "For every day could be the last." Now and then they draw the red checked kitchen curtains aside and look out to see whether there are Signs in the Heavens.

No, not yet. There is only darkness and the whispering waters and the lantern in the Redoubt.

It happens that a strange light can be seen in the sky, as though something very big is approaching bathed in light. But then it's only the Moon rising behind the horizon.

Fina the Hut

The Wise Virgins are sisters. They are not only wise, but they are also good, for they want to help to save everyone from damnation on the Last Day. So they go around proclaiming the words of the Scriptures.

Most of all they would like to save Fina the Hut, for Fina is their very own sister. But she is a poor child of sin.

Fina doesn't live together with her sisters; she has her own house. It is known as the Hut. People turn their noses up at the Hut. It's a small whitewashed house with partly tarred walls and a turf roof, and it stands in the middle of a lovely garden full of flowering bushes and green vegetables.

Here live Fina and her daughter Rosa, who is known as Dolly Rose because she looks like a doll, a red and white doll of the kind that can close its eyes when it is laid down. Dolly Rose's cheeks are red like redcurrants, and her eyes the colour of gooseberries. She always dresses in her Sunday best. She often stands by the gate of the Hut garden, staring up in the air with her big doll's eyes.

Fina the Hut makes a living from her garden, selling flowers and green vegetables to people. And she makes wreaths and helps at weddings and funerals. And she can foresee the future and conjure spirits and "play tricks" with people she doesn't like. So everyone is nice and kind to Fina and her Dolly Rose, for they are afraid of having a spell cast on them.

The chervils in the Hut garden are full of white flowery hands that all clutch at the wind. In one corner of the garden there is a bed full of flaming red poppies. If you stand and stare long enough into the red blaze of flowers, you *lose yourself*.

There are long, dangerous claws on Fina's hoe, which is

left in the dark green bed of parsley.

Fina the Hut herself is small and neat, with rosy cheeks and a nice smile on her lips and often with a dewdrop on the end of her nose. She hands you the bunch of parsley with the curly leaves and accepts her few coins, and perhaps she will pat your head and bless you, and then you can feel her dangerous hoe-like fingers in your hair for the rest of the day.

In the evening, when the blaze of poppies has been extinguished and the dusk is like a green lake between the tall chervils, the lamp is lit behind the curtains in the windows of the Hut. Then you can see a big bird standing in the garden flapping its wings and shaking earth and dust from its feathers, and then Fina opens her window and smiles sweetly at the black bird and lets it into her kitchen.

"Who's telling you all those tall stories about Fina, Amaldus?"

"Nobody."

"Well, it's all a lot of nonsense, for Fina's no witch, but a nice, kind little person."

Silence.

"Why does Fina have a dewdrop on the end of her nose?"

"It's because evil tongues are so busy telling stories about her."

But Fina the Hut *is* a witch even so. And perhaps her Dolly Rose is a princess under a spell. And perhaps a prince will come one day and free her from Fina's hoe-like claws.

The Old Poet

In that tall house on the slope near the lake lives The Old Poet.

The Old Poet's thin face is yellow like faded paper. His mouth is hidden beneath a silvery white beard. His eyebrows are two black tufts. They shoot right up into his forehead when he's thinking.

He speaks only rarely, but he coughs a lot, for he has consumption. He always wears a slight smile. "He wonders at the world."

He pats your cheek with a veined hand and he winks at you as though you have a secret together, but he doesn't say much.

The place where the Old Poet's house stands used long ago to be a churchyard. In his vestibule he has a barrel full of the dead people's bones that he has gathered while digging his garden. There are skulls, too, with dark eye sockets and big grinning teeth. The Old Poet has painted a black cross on the barrel. So it's a holy barrel.

The mouldy bones are in their holy barrel waiting for the Last Day, when they will arise and turn into living people again.

Then they will come and press the Old Poet's hand and say thank you to him for his kindness, and he will smile to them and say, "Don't mention it."

Howler Hans

One house is neither tarred nor painted and doesn't have grass on the roof like other houses in town, but is unpainted and has a roof of iron. This is where the furious man Howler Hans lives.

Howler Hans is small, broad-shouldered and bald. His nostrils are big and open. His eyes are blood red.

Howler Hans isn't his real name, but a nickname.

Howler Hans lives alone in his house. His wife Anna Diana had to run away from him with her two children, for he is dangerous when he is in a temper.

Howler Hans stands in his doorway and talks or sings. He talks of Judgement Day and the Great Beast that will rise from the sea and of the evil spirit that entered the herd of swine. Sometimes he just grins or roars.

Sometimes Howler Hans rages in his empty house and breaks everything and throws saucepans and chair legs out of the window.

Howler Hans is not like that all the time, however, and when he is free from the evil spirit that rages in him, he works decently in the quarry, where the stones for the new savings bank are blasted out of the rock face.

But one day a package full of dynamite was found to have disappeared from the quarry, and so the alarm was raised and Howler Hans' house was searched from attic to cellar, for the previous evening someone had seen the crazy fellow leaving the quarry carrying a square package in a sack on his back. That was the package of dynamite.

That package was never found, although Howler Hans later confessed that he was the one who had taken it and hidden it in his cellar. So people went around for a long time afraid of some nasty accident happening.

But then, one early morning, while Howler Hans was still asleep in bed, six serious men came and fetched him. He was bound fast on a ladder and carried out to the Madhouse. There, he could be heard singing and shouting behind the iron bars on the tiny windows.

The strong man known as China Hans, who looks after the lunatics, says that Howler Hans has torn all his clothes off and goes about naked, fighting and biting at the evil spirit that has taken possession of him, and that he is so sweaty that he slips out of your grasp like a slippery fish if you try to catch him.

***

The minister came one day and said a prayer over Howler Hans, but he couldn't cast out the evil spirit. Fina the Hut is the only person who can do that, but she isn't allowed, because she "does magic".

One evening, China Hans nevertheless sent for the girl from the Hut. She came with a bag of green leaves that she stuck on the madman's wet forehead.

Then he fell quiet for a week, but on the evening of the seventh day, he was dead.

The Sorrows of Little Brother

The porcelain dog, "White Freja" is white with some gilt on it, and it is so big that you can sit and ride on its back. But it is usually to be found at the bottom of a cupboard and it only sees the light of day when the Wise Virgins are there on a visit. For it was a wedding present from the Virgins and they mustn't know that it is usually hidden away in the cupboard.

"But why does it have to be in the cupboard?"

That question doesn't produce a real answer. Mother wrinkles her nose a little. Little Brother can get the porcelain doll out and have it to play with.

Little Brother is now so big that he can sit and ride on the fine dog, for which we think of a name, calling it after the poodle known as Freja that belongs to Lambertsen the watchmaker. But since Lambertsen's Freja is black, ours is called "White Freja".

On White Freja's back you can ride out into the "wide world", which we imagine is a white world with some gilt in it. Everything in this white world is white and shiny and sparkling, but as fragile as glass. All the houses are white, but they have gilt roofs and doors, and all trees and bushes are white, but they have leaves of gold.

This is a game for rainy weather and it's only played on dark and wet days when you can't play out of doors.

On the shelf above the chest of drawers there are three white ladies with no clothes on, and they are the "Three Graces". They look very fine, but there is something not quite right about them, for their willies are missing. And not only are the three ladies naked, but they are blind as well, for they have no dots in their eyes to see with.

Little Brother wonders at that. But then he goes on riding on White Freja's back through that strange white world where everything is shiny and stiff and polished and full of things that are strangely not there.

Little Brother loves White Freja and kisses her gilt snout. But one day a dreadful thing happens: White Freja falls down and is broken. Then all that is left of her lies scattered on the floor in broken pieces of white and gilt, all shiny and golden on the outside but grey on the inside, and then Little Brother starts crying and can't be comforted. For now White Freja is dead and it's he who has killed her. It's no use Mother taking him on her lap and saying that it wasn't done on purpose and that it doesn't really matter and that Little Brother can have a rocking horse instead of White Freja, or perhaps a real doggy. There is no end to Little Brother's bitter tears. Upset and horrified he looks at the sharp fragments that Aunt Nanna is sweeping up. – White Freja's gilt ear and pieces of her paws and tail.

When the Wise Virgins came on their next visit and saw no sign of their wedding present, Mother had to tell a lie and say that the beautiful dog had fallen down off the chest of drawers and that she was really sorry about that.

Then the Virgins gave a kindly smile and brushed it aside.

"Oh, there are far worse things than that, dear. And now it won't be long before we ourselves fall to pieces, and that will be the end of us all in this vale of tears."

Stare-Eyes in the Snow

But the white glass world hasn't quite crumbled away. The winter brings it back.

Winter has come, icicles are hanging from every eave, the snow swirls through streets and alleyways, and strange pictures appear on the windows, pictures of lovely shining gardens in which all branches and leaves are of glass.

They are ice flowers. Frost has drawn them.

Frost, that strange lanky figure with the long arms and the big red flapping ears, rushes around in the dark, or perhaps in the moonlight and the Northern Lights; with busy fingers he draws his array of pictures on all the windows.

In the frosty gardens it's as quiet as in the churchyard. But if you listen you can hear they are alive with a gentle ringing as though of a host of tiny distant bells. This is the sound of silence. It is the sound behind all sounds.

But out on Our Lady's Hill there is a throng of sledges and skis and wagon seats and shouts and cries of "Mind out! Out of the way!"

"Stay away from Our Lady's Hill, Amaldus. It's too dangerous for children of your age. You stay on the Lamb Slope."

But the Lamb Slope is boring, for the only ones sledging here are little children who daren't join in on Our Lady's Hill, and so you nevertheless make your way out there to the big, dangerous slope with your sledge.

And – hey – you're off at a terrific speed down the steep hill and far out on the frozen lake known as the Abbatjørn.

Once, twice all goes well, but things go wrong the third time: you are run into by another, much bigger sledge and you come to grief and are swallowed up in a deep snow drift and you get your mouth and eyes full of snow. But the other sledge has come to grief as well, and you are not the only one to be digging yourself out of the white drifts, for the snow is full of heads and hands, and everyone is whining and roaring with laughter. And then: *"Hello. Amaldus!"* someone shouts, and it is none other than Stare-Eyes. But she is so covered in snow that you hardly recognise her. But then someone calls out, *"Come on, Merrit."* And then Stare-Eyes is gone again, and you stand there wondering that she is called Merrit and that she knows your name...

***

Your names encountered each other briefly there in the drifting snow, one white winter's day long, long go. Then she disappeared in snow and dusk. But wait, she'll be back, for *Merrit* has come into your life now...

Black Christmas

Now comes a time of gales and cloudbursts; the snow melts and is gone within a single night. All the slopes are transformed into raging torrents and the river through the town into a heavy, gurgling river. Christmas is not white, but wet and black.

And on Christmas Night itself, the entire town was awakened by a clap of thunder that shook every house.

The Tower at the Edge of the World

Only a single clap of thunder, if it *was* a clap of thunder, for in the clap there was also a sound like bells complaining...

It turned out that the lightning had struck the church tower.

A bad sign! The tower was all black on one side, as though it had been licked by a giant, sooty tongue, and the cross at the top of the spire was all skew-whiff. And the church clock had stopped and was showing five minutes past three. Fearful forces had been at play. But they had nevertheless not been able to set fire to the tower or to destroy the bell. And even though they had managed to bend the sacred cross, they hadn't managed to break it off.

The vicar's Christmas sermon is about that, and in great exultation the congregation sing the joyful words:

Full many a tower may crumble and fall,
But bells still survive and ring out and call.

And on New Year's Eve the tower was painted a beautiful white again and there it stands beneath nascent Northern Lights, and the cross has been straightened out again.

But during the coming days, strange stories were told about the fear and commotion occasioned by the strange lightning strike. Many people had almost been out of their minds with fear. The Wise Virgins had behaved in a completely crazy manner, standing outside on the steps leading up to their door, singing and holding lighted candles in their hands.

And then, down in the Coffee House Aunt Nanna had heard Spanish Rikke talking about a great quarrel there had been in the Hut between the Virgins and Fina and which had ended with Fina threatening her sisters with a pair of garden shears and shouting, "*I'll* show you signs in the heavens if you don't buzz off!"

Father (with a hearty laugh): "Aye, if it really was Fina the Hut who was responsible for that thunder clap, I take my hat off to her!"

The Almanac

The cover of the Almanac is framed with tiny pictures: lions and bulls, fish and crabs, people and horses, and one that is half a man and half a horse and is shooting a bow and arrow.

The Almanac contains a list of all the days, including the days that haven't come yet. Every day is someone's birthday. All the days have strange names.

"What's today called?"

Mother, who is writing a letter to her sister Helene in Copenhagen, looks it up in the Almanac: "Saint Polycarp".

"And tomorrow?"

"Chrysostomus".

"Have all the days always been there?"

"No, for one day was the first day of Creation. That's when God created light."

"But will there always be new days?"

"No, for one day will be the Last Day. The Last Day is Judgement Day. That's God's day."

"Then won't there be any more days after Judgement Day?"

"No, then there will only be one long day that lasts forever."

"But when there's no more night, will people never sleep?"

Mother shakes her head, looks up at the ceiling and smiles.

"Heavens above, boy, what a lot of things you ask about! Will people sleep after Judgement Day?"

Then Mother bends over her letter: "I must write and tell Auntie Helene about that."

"Tell her what?"

"That you are asking whether there will be any sleeping after Judgement Day."

***

But then it *is* the sole long and everlasting day after Judgement Day...

Then there is no sun, but only a desolate light as it were coming from all around. And there isn't a single human being left in the whole world, and no animals and no grass, not even as much as a single withered blade. And in the sand down by the vast motionless ocean there isn't a sign of a single bird. But there are some scattered fragments here and there of a smashed earthenware jar and a broken pipe and a cracked mirror. And a ball-like herring net buoy of green glass.

And you yourself are a transparent green glass bird hovering low over the sand on fine, delicate glass wings.

The bird flies away faster and faster – but where, where?

Towards the Edge of the Abyss.

Here, the green bird flies more slowly and stops – here at the Furthermost Edge, where the Tower rises, huge and dark, craggy and grey like a mountain top, and the huge windows right up at the very top stare at you black and empty – like the eye sockets in the dead men's skulls in the Old Poet's barrel. It is such an overpowering sight that the green bird has to screech – big, green, tormented glass screeches.

There is someone moving far out in Eternity: a big, eiderdown-like cloud comes slowly floating along. But it's no cloud, for now you can clearly see that it has both a face and hands.

It's God hovering above the waters. He's coming closer

and closer, and it's terrible...

But then you wake up in your bed, bathed in sweat.

And now it is early morning on Earth and in Normality; the window panes are turning blue in the daylight, and out in the kitchen, where the lamp is lit, your quite ordinary mother is busy filtering the coffee.

"You look upset, Amaldus. Have you had a nasty dream again?"

"Yes. All about the time after the end of the world."

"Oh, and what was it like?"

Then you tell her about your dream, in general terms, about the green glass bird and the Edge of the Abyss and the huge tower with the skull at the top and about God who came along like a floating eiderdown.

Mother is busy and only half listens to your shocking account.

"Well, you often dream such funny things. But you'll soon forget it, for dreams are only a funny kind of hocus-pocus."

That was the usual comment from the grown-ups when you told them about your dreams. And it made you feel silly and you preferred to keep your dreams to yourself.

Uncle Harry

Aunt Nanna is more radiant than ever, for now she has got engaged. Her fiancé is called Harry; he's a sailor and sails on the sloop the *Queen Mary*.

As soon as the *Queen Mary* has dropped anchor in the roads, Uncle Harry rows ashore and hurries across to kiss Aunt Nanna. He simply can't wait.

Then Aunt Nanna hides in the cellar or in some corner of the garden and blushes, for she doesn't like others to see how

Uncle Harry kisses her, and she's also a bit afraid of him, 'cos he wears sea boots and a greatcoat and a fur cap and he has a big beard and "eyes like a hungry wolf". He doesn't say hello, for he simply can't talk, only puff.

"Nanna! Nanna!"

Uncle Harry comes back later, and now he has had a shave and is well dressed, wearing a hat and a dickey bow tie with a watch chain and cigar holder and a rose in his buttonhole and blue tattoos on his wrist, and now he can speak and laugh like everyone else.

But Aunt Nanna still doesn't really like him to have his arm round her waist or neck all the time, and so she blows at his face and looks as though she's tired of him.

Besides, she thinks he is too old to carry on in such a silly way, for he's thirty years old. And they aren't married, only engaged.

In the evenings they sit on the sofa in the dark living room, and then you can only see the glow of Uncle Harry's cigar and hear a few sounds of whispering. But sometimes Uncle Harry will sing with a warm, trembling voice, and then it is always something touching that makes Aunt Nanna sigh and sob, especially when he sings:

And who can forget the dearest one of all?

But one day, the *Queen Mary* returned without Uncle Harry.

Where is Uncle Harry now? He's not dead. He's in England. He no longer sails on the *Queen Mary*, but on an English ship.

One day, Aunt Nanna received a letter from England, and then she was not seen for several days, but sat alone in her room. She was not in bed, but simply sitting on a chair. Neither did she weep. She was simply overcome.

When she appeared again, Aunt Nanna was pale and downcast, and she was no longer radiant and she said not a word.

Then that winter passed.

But one day, who should come rushing through the garden in a greatcoat and with a full beard? Uncle Harry! His eyes are full of tears, and he can't talk, only puff, "Nanna, Nanna."

But Aunt Nanna flees to her room and locks the door.

Uncle Harry stood for a long time knocking and weeping at the locked door until Mother came and spoke to him seriously:

"I think you should leave, Harry, for you are a *feckless idiot.*"

Then Uncle Harry threw his arms round Mother's neck so she had to sit down, and then he knelt and wept with his head on her lap. But none of this was any use. Father turned up and gave him a thorough dressing down and then showed the feckless idiot the door.

Bowed down and sobbing loudly, Uncle Harry stumbled out through the garden, while up in her room, Aunt Nanna sat sobbing.

The Poppies

In the corner of the Hut garden, where the red poppies stand resplendent in the summer, there is only black earth during the winter. But new poppies are on the way, and each time you go past the Hut garden you look at the poppy bed to see whether anything is starting to happen.

Then, one day there is a tiny eye to be seen. A hard, white eye in the black earth.

Then, in the coming days, some pale fingers come into view, pushing their way forward with eager knuckles and growing and developing into bulging shoots.

Then it's spring.

Then, one day, some shaggy buds have raised their whiskered heads from the green confusion. They stand there holding tight on to something they don't want to let go of.

But see, a curly red creature peeps out of the cracks in the fierce buds. Then it looks as though they have been wounded and are bleeding.

But then, suddenly, the poppies have unfolded their flaming red tops and stand there gently waving in the wind, so fiery red, so fiery red in all the greenery.

Then it is summer.

The Organ Grinder

Something remarkable happened that summer: an organ grinder came to town.

Was that really so remarkable? Yes, for us children, who had never seen an organ grinder before or heard a barrel organ, it was an event.

No one knew where he came from, but it was said that a Norwegian ship on its way to Iceland had put him ashore because he had no money to pay for his journey. But there he was: suddenly, one sunny summer afternoon this organ grinder was standing out in the middle of Doctor Square grinding his barrel organ, and on top of the organ there was a little monkey dressed up as a lady in a frock and bonnet and wearing a pair of light blue glasses. And it could dance a little and blow kisses.

The organ grinder was neither Norwegian nor Icelandic, and neither was he Danish – but there were those who said that he might have come from Spain or Turkey, or perhaps he was a gypsy. He was a pathetic figure to see, with a yellowish face and a hump back, with a black beard and a black patch over one eye, and several people came along and put a few coins in the old hat standing on the ground in front of the barrel organ. But no one, not even the little children, could really enjoy his music because he looked so pitiful. Nor was there anyone who would have him living in their home because he might carry some infection and, besides, he might steal from them.

Then Mother went into action and gave the organ grinder a place to live in our cellar; he was given a bed to sleep in and plenty to eat and drink, both for himself and his monkey. He also had his old patched jersey exchanged for one of Father's discarded jackets, and he was so grateful and he bowed courteously like a man who had known better days. But then he fell ill and had to stay in his bed. And Doctor Fridericia was sent for, but he couldn't find anything particularly wrong with the foreign visitor.

"He's just pretty wretched and needs looking after a bit, but the way you are feeding him he'll soon recover."

And the organ grinder really did recover and get a warm glow in his cheeks and a gleam in the eye that could see, and there was no end to his gratitude. There was no one who really understood what he said in that foreign language of his, but that they were words of praise was obvious from his eyes and the caressing movements of his long hands. Finally, he was able to come up from his cellar and to sit at the kitchen table and have his meals there together with his little monkey lady. He began to look better, and you could see that in spite of his hump he was a quite good-looking and decent person with nice laughter lines around his eyes and lovely splashes of silver in his coal black beard. It was also revealed that the organ grinder could do more than play his barrel organ. He was good at riveting. He was able to fix the Three Graces that had fallen down from the shelf so well that they looked like new, and he took a dirty old dish that had long been lying upside down in the slush in the poultry run, cleaning it and polishing it and as though by magic transforming it into a shining copper bowl. And he could also carve patterns in wood and make little figures and funny dolls from seaweed fronds that we children brought to him.

A couple of weeks passed in this way in peace and quiet until Father came home on the *Christina*, at which time it all came to a sudden end. It turned out that Father could understand quite a lot of the organ grinder's language. They talked for a long time together alone down in the stranger's cellar room, and it didn't sound nice: Father banged on the table, and it sounded as though the organ grinder was moaning and pleading.

When Father emerged from the cellar again, his hands were shaking and his cheeks flushed, but he said nothing. Mother took him in both her arms, and she, too, was very upset and had tears in her eyes.

"But what on earth *was* it, Johan?"

Father took her aside and whispered something in her ear.

Mother stood with her eyes closed and looked as though she had turned to stone.

Then no more happened, and everything seemed to be as before except that the organ grinder no longer emerged from his room. Father let one of the assistants in the shop take his food down to him.

Shortly after this, the organ grinder left on board the *Christina*, which was carrying a cargo of fish to Spain. Now he looked quite different from when he came, dressed as he was in a decent jersey and wearing a seaman's cap with a shiny peak, but the strangest thing of all was that not only was the black eye patch gone, but his hump had also quite disappeared.

He had the little monkey in a shawl in his arm. In the vestibule he quickly kissed Mother's and Aunt Nanna's sleeves. When he had gone, Mother sat for a long time hiding her face in her hands.

It was a curious event that reminded you of all those strange things that happen in fairy tales or dreams, and you were not much the wiser from the explanation you got from Aunt Nanna.

"Your father didn't like him. Couldn't stand him."

"Yes, but why?"

"Because he was a poor *feckless idiot*."

"What's a feckless idiot?"

Aunt Nanna doesn't answer that, but just puffs you in the face.

"And because your father's a *tyrant*."

"Tyrant? What's a tyrant?"

She doesn't answer that either, but simply stands there flushed and with anger in her eyes and with her mouth twisted as though in disgust.

Grey, Windy Winter's Day with no Sun or Shade.

An ordinary day. A day late in time.

Here, from the tower when I, Amaldus the Ageing Reminiscer, am now sitting (well, *tower* is perhaps saying too much, for we are talking of a sorely modest cabin where, in addition to myself as I write, there is only room for a table and a chair and a little fireplace and, under the table, a folded parachute) – from the window up here in my elevated nook I can sit and look out across the tiny smoke-veiled town in the midst of the ocean, where three quarters of a century ago I saw the light of day and the darkness of night for the first time and had my first timorous thoughts about life and death – thoughts that have perhaps since taken on a more clearly definable shape, but which are no less helpless for that...

Here I sit, staring far out into the distance, out into the Land of Youth, gone and for ever vanished, a place to which I no longer belong, and which I secretly envy you who still have a free rein down there; especially I envy you your wonderful regenerative ability!

Down there, where the beginning began and the continuation still continues, night and day still pursue their customary course, everyday reality still reigns, life is lived, those great things that are worth experiencing are still experienced, those landmark first things that ever make life constantly new.

From this long *cri de coeur* it might be understood that the town of which we are talking is not a voluntary refuge, but a prison, the miserable cell of age and corruption at the End of the World. Aye, here I sit abandoned in my lofty prison on the edge of the great abyss – listening to the threatening roar from the depths and trying to take the situation with good grace, although God (who still hovers like a cloud above the waters) knows that it is not always easy and that it would be quite unbearable if I couldn't cheat a bit.

So look, I will take my good parachute out now and open the window, and then I will float slowly and full of delicious expectations down to the vanished but imperishable places where my heart is at home.

Hannibal

Then it was that one day I fell among thieves and got to know Hannibal...

On the little stretch of sand below the warehouses at the mouth of the river running through the town, where you had gone to sail your two toy boats, the *Christina* and the *Sea Serpent*, a lot of empty packing cases had been piled one on top of the other so they looked like a tower. There was a little peephole in one of them, and up there an observant face appeared, then other suspicious faces with watchful eyes, and suddenly a bunch of wild savages issues from this peculiar tower, and before you can manage to get away you are grabbed and put into a narrow, dark cell. Here you lie wriggling and doing your best to resist and kick down the sides of the packing case while plaintively shouting, "Give me my ships back." But your complaints meet only with silence. Then a voice is heard:

"You're a prisoner. If you don't shut up, you'll be shot."

"Give me my ships."

"We're going to burn them."

Then you do the silliest thing possible – you start to cry. You sob aloud and cry out while furiously stamping on the floor and battering the sides.

Then a gap opens in the top and you get a glimpse of hands and grinning faces, and one of your ships is lowered down to you. It's the *Christina* with the white sails. But before you can grab it, it's pulled up again, and this is repeated time after time to the accompaniment of suppressed laughter.

Then the laughter suddenly stops, and a pistol appears in the hole above.

"Beg for mercy."

"Let me out."

"Beg for mercy, or else you'll be shot."

"I want out."

"Beg for mercy. I'll count to three. *One!*"

"Let me out."

"Beg for mercy. *Two!*"

"No, don't."

"Three!"

Then the pistol is fired and you get a sharp jet of water straight in your face. It hits your nose and mouth and makes you sneeze and splutter."

"Now will you beg for mercy?"

Well, you beg for mercy, for you are no hero.

So you've begged for mercy and you are let out of the cell and you are sitting on the floor of a rather bigger and lighter packing-case cell, wet and embarrassed and furious, but quite broken.

"You could have begged for mercy straight away, Amaldus, and then you wouldn't have been shot."

The voice is that of a redheaded boy whom you know to be called Hannibal and who is the son of the widow Anna Diana, the woman who has been married to Howler Hans. He is a couple of years older than you and is very big for his age. He is wearing a dark green waistcoat over his jersey and there is a watch chain with a compass suspended between the two pockets of his waistcoat, while a dagger hangs at his belt in a shining wooden sheath.

"And here are your rotten ships. Now go home and tell tales, you weakling."

This was your first encounter with Hannibal.

You stayed where you were, embittered and humiliated, with five or six robbers' eyes staring at your feeble person. You stayed there without taking your ships and going off.

You asked for mercy, you were humiliated, but you stayed where you were, for you didn't want to be a weakling.

Embarrassed silence. Hannibal still sits there with one of your ships on his knees; it's the *Sea Serpent.* He sits stroking the lovely ship with the gilt prow.

"You're a queer fish, Amaldus. Who made these ships for you? Your father?"

"Ole Morske."

Silence. Murmuring. "Ole Morske."

"Like a cigarette, Amaldus?"

"No."

He lights a cigarette for himself and sits there blowing smoke rings.

"Have you really had your ships out sailing in salt water?"

"No, only up in the river."

Hannibal suddenly gets up.

"Come with me, Amaldus."

And to the others, who show signs of preparing to come with us, "No, 'cos Amaldus and I are going alone. Aren't we, Amaldus? I want to talk to you about something."

He turns round and beckons to one of the boys: "*You* can come, Karl-Erik."

We go out along the shore to the little bay called The Bight, Hannibal and I each carrying a ship in our arms. And we set the ships sailing out here in the calm waters in the cove. There is no wind; there they lie rocking, reflected in the water; the afternoon sun blazes down on the white sails of the *Christina* and the rust-coloured ones of the *Sea Serpent*. Hannibal and I sit there for a while looking at each other in silence while Karl-Erik keeps an eye on the ships. Hannibal's face is covered with freckles except for a spot on one cheek, where there is a white scar. He has a front tooth missing. His eyes are small and pale.

"Are you still mad with us, Amaldus?"

"Me? No."

"Did you think I was going to steal your ships?"

"Yes."

"Aye. I think the others were going to. But then I *forbade* them. 'Cos I'm the *chieftain*."

Hannibal tosses his head a little and adopts a stern look. He's the chieftain and all the others must obey him.

"Were you terribly frightened when you were going to be shot? Did you think it was a real pistol?"

"Yes."

Hannibal takes the pistol out.

"It's a jolly nice pistol, isn't it? Everyone's frightened of it even though it only shoots water. And you can put salt or vinegar in the water, and then it *burns*."

He whistles through his fingers: "Hey, Karl-Erik. Go and fill the pistol."

Hannibal hands me the filled pistol. "Look, press it there."

The big iron-grey pistol looks quite formidable, but when you hold it in your hand and feel the rubber, it is nothing but a fake after all. Hannibal takes it back and shoots a lovely long jet of water up in the air.

"Hey, Amaldus. What would you say to letting me have one of your ships and you having this? Is that a bargain? Yes or no?"

"No."

Hannibal looks as though this was the answer he had been expecting. But then he takes the dagger out of its fine sheath and sits and makes it shine in the sun.

"But what do you say to having this in exchange? It's a good dagger. It's very sharp. You can cut a cockerel's head off with it. And you could stab someone to death with it. So what do you say, Amaldus? Yes or no?"

"No."

"Well, it'd be daft of you to say yes, Amaldus, but then I was only asking you to test you – to find out whether you're

60

stupid or clever. But see here."

Hannibal takes a pocket watch out of his waistcoat pocket. It is set in a yellow, worn horn case. He opens the case and lets the big, shiny pocket watch dangle from the chain.

"This is an expensive watch. It's an *heirloom*. So what do you say now, Amaldus? Yes or no?"

"You can have the *Sea Serpent* for nothing if you want."

"For nothing?"

"Yes, for nothing."

"Well, just you think carefully, Amaldus. I'll count to fifty while you think."

Hannibal turns away so as not to disturb me while I think."

"Well? Do you still say that?"

"Yes."

Hannibal does a finger whistle. "Come over here, Karl-Erik, I want you to be a witness."

Now the promise has to be repeated while Karl-Erik listens to it.

"Go down and fetch the ships," commands Hannibal.

He nudges me: "Karl-Erik's my servant, my *hajduk*. He's a nice little chap, but it's a pity for him 'cos he's going to die soon."

"Why?"

"'Cos he's got *consumption*. All his brothers and sisters have died of consumption, all of them except his youngest sister, but she's ill and she's going to die as well soon."

Karl-Erik comes with the ships, and Hannibal puts the *Sea Serpent* on his knee and strokes it with delight.

"That was wise of you, Amaldus. 'Cos you wouldn't have got that expensive watch in any case, you know. But I'll still give you something in exchange. I've made my mind up on that. I know what. It's something you'll like. You will. But it's got to be seen in a certain way. It's only good when you see it in a certain way. If you come down here tomorrow and the weather's good, you'll be able to see it."

"See what?"

"I'm not going to tell you now. But you'll like it a lot, Amaldus, I know you will. See, shake hands to be sure I'm not going to cheat you. And Karl-Erik, you're a *witness*."

Hannibal gives me a firm handshake to ensure that I won't be cheated.

"And now we're friends, Amaldus. We are friends, aren't we? Yes or no?"

"Yes."

Hannibal looks intently at me. Then he sits down for a moment and strokes the *Sea Serpent* and looks as though he was going to say something but doesn't quite dare.

"You're not the least bit mad at me now, Amaldus, are you?"

"No."

"Look, Amaldus, shall I tell you something you don't know?"

"Yes?"

"Then I can tell you that you're almost my brother. At least you're my cousin. You didn't know that, did you?"

"No."

"Well, let me explain. Do you want me to explain it to you?"

"Yes."

"Well, my mother's your grandfather's daughter, the grandfather that had the same name as you. So now you know, Amaldus. So your mother and my mother are sisters, see? So they're both equally good, aren't they? Aren't they Amaldus? Yes or no."

"I suppose so."

Hannibal sits rocking the *Sea Serpent* on his knees. He holds the ship up towards the sun so that the light shines through the red sails.

"Are you mad at me, Amaldus? Yes, you are. I can see it in you."

"Me? No."

"No, but you're not very happy either. But in any case it doesn't matter, 'cos you'll *be* happy when you get my present. I'll guarantee that."

***

The following day we met again at the Bight; there was a bright autumn sunshine and a cold wind.

"Come on. Now you're going to see it."

"See what?"

"Get a move on."

"Where are we going?"

"Up to Our Lady's Hill."

We hurry away. Up on Our Lady's Hill there is a crowd of boys, all looking up at the sky.

"Can you see it now, Amaldus?"

"Yes, a kite. Is it yours?"

"Yes, but it's yours now. I've made it myself. You can see it's not any old kite, 'cos it's all gold. Can you see it's gold all over its head, Amaldus? And can you see its eyes?"

Yes, you can see that its head shines all gold and has big white eyes with black dots in them and red tufts for its ears.

It was a clear and sunny, but perishing cold day in October with frost and a north wind, but it was one of those days you don't forget. The big paper kite stood out sparkling against the pale sky, with its long tail slowly flapping like a fish swimming free in the water and waggling its tail. (There are really few sights on earth that can compete in gracefulness with the sight of the excited but elegant and leisurely movements of a kite's tail.)

Hannibal passed to you the reel to which the string was fastened.

"Just feel how it *pulls!*"

Indeed it pulled. It was just like having a huge fish on a hook.

There we spent all that long afternoon *enjoying* the kite dancing high up in the low, cold sunshine and never tiring of playing and doing all kinds of celestial hops, skips and jumps. With us down on earth, dusk gradually fell, but up there where the kite was, it was still day for a long time.

Only when the dusk became more intense and the stars began to shine did Hannibal reel in the line holding the kite, slowly, for there was no hurry, and the kite didn't like it; it pitched and tossed and grew ever more unreasonable as it came closer to the ground, and when finally it lay on the grass like a pile of tinsel and newspaper through which the wind was whistling, everything became so strangely sad. No one said anything. Hannibal wrapped the long paper tail around the head of the kite and fixed the reel to the crossbeam, and then there was only a deep and lonely evening with stars and Northern Lights and a cold that made your teeth chatter.

Hannibal handed the folded kite to me.

"Well, aren't you pleased with this fine present, Amaldus?"

"Yes."

"Well, then, I think you should say thank you."

The Skull

Hannibal isn't one you can play around with. Either you are his friend, in which case everything is fine, or else you are his enemy, in which case Heaven help you. But if you want to be his friend, you have to have a cut made in your finger and mix your blood with his.

"Will you? Well, it does hurt a bit. But say whether you will or not. Well? Yes or no?"

"Yes, but not today."

Hannibal puts on a chieftain's look.

"It's got to be today or never."

"Well, then I don't want to."

"Oh, so you're scared? Oh well. So was I at your age. But then I pulled myself together, 'cos I didn't want to be a coward any longer."

So we mix our blood after all.

It all takes place in the cellar beneath the "Chapterhouse", one of the dilapidated old warehouses near the Square. This is where Hannibal has his "robbers' den". This is where, well hidden in a wooden box and wrapped in hessian, he has his *maroon*, a large and tightly packed and tarred package, out of which projects the end of a fuse. With this maroon he could blow the entire warehouse up if he wanted, indeed even set fire to the whole town. But he doesn't want to. At least not yet.

The mixing of blood doesn't hurt as much as might be expected. Hannibal's dagger is big and sharp, but it only makes a quite small cut in the soft flesh at the tip of the little finger, and then a drop of blood comes out, and that's enough. It is wiped off with the blade of the knife and flicked down into a chipped saucer and mixed in salt water together with a much bigger drop of Hannibal's blood.

"Now you've got to say the Our Father backwards."

"Well, I'm not going to."

"Yes, come on."

"No, I won't."

Hannibal smiles and reveals his funny teeth with one front tooth missing and another black.

"It's a *good thing* that you won't, Amaldus. You mustn't tempt God. And I only said it to test you. But you'll have to kiss the skull. Come on."

At the foot of the slope beneath the Old Poet's House there lies a pile of rubbish scattered on the little foreshore, pieces of seaweed and splintered bits of wood, dried jellyfish and bits of glass, rusty saucepans and other discarded kitchen utensils. There are also some bones that the surf has washed down from the old cemetery up on the slope. And, well hidden in a pile of brushwood and gravel, there is a skull, which Hannibal takes out and brushes and polishes.

"Here, kiss its forehead."

"No, I won't."

"Now, now. But you see, Amaldus, if you won't, then you can expect the dead man to come back and visit you tonight."

"Well, I'm still not going to."

Hannibal stands there polishing the greenish skull with the sleeve of his jersey. It looks so grisly that you get cold shivers down your spine. He bends his head down and gives you a piercing and imperious look.

"You *must*, Amaldus."

"No. You can kiss it yourself if you want to."

But then comes the sound of a gentle but plaintive voice from the top of the slope. It's the old poet, who is leaning on a spade and has a big, woollen scarf wrapped around his neck and beard. He has stood there and seen it all.

"What are you doing, boys? Come and give me that thing you're holding, Hannibal."

Hannibal hesitates; he stands hugging the skull and looking sombre and defiant.

"Come on, lads, both of you." The voice is heard again from the top of the slope, this time very insistent.

Hannibal's eyes grow dark. "Now you're going to keep quiet about everything, Amaldus. Promise?"

The poet takes the skull and examines it as he holds it out in front of him.

"What are you going to do with it, boys?"

No answer.

"It's probably the head of a young girl. Just look how delicately it's shaped. And the little teeth are almost all there. What a pity the council still leaves all these poor human remains lying around like any other bits of rubbish."

He looks at us with big, open eyes and with his black eyebrows drawn high up in his forehead.

"Are you really playing with the poor *cranium*? It's not a toy, lads, it's the skull of someone who was perhaps your age and perhaps played out here like you."

(Perhaps it's Lonela's head, you thought).

The poet looks at us a little longer. Then he sighs and gently takes the skull as though wanting to protect it and, coughing slightly, goes up towards his house. We see him open the cellar door and disappear into the darkness of the vestibule, where he has his strange bin of bones standing.

Hannibal shrugs his shoulders.

"Well, that's up to him. Oh well, but all that about kissing the skull was only to test you."

***

The wind has started blowing, and it's kite weather. Perhaps there's a bit too much wind. But even so we decide to fetch the kite.

On the way we go past the Hut garden and here stands Dolly Rose at the gate, smiling and looking up in the air as though she was smiling to someone far away. She is neatly dressed as always, with a chequered bonnet and a decorative apron.

Hannibal: "Hello, Rosie"

"Hello."

Rose's voice is curiously faint, as though not quite real, and her big brown doll's eyes don't move, but still stare into the distance. Hannibal goes close to her and whispers, "What have you had for dinner today, Dolly? Have you eaten your black cat?"

Rose makes no reply, but smiles and shows a row of wet teeth between her thick lips.

But now the voice of Fina the Hut is heard from somewhere or other: *"I heard you, Hannibal."*

And now she appears behind some shrubbery, holding a rake from the teeth of which she is pulling some roots. She is smiling politely but with her eyes averted.

"Are you going looking for dead crows for supper, my boy?"

Hannibal makes no reply, but stands and swallows.

"Come on, Amaldus."

***

That afternoon saw the tragedy of the fine, gilt kite breaking lose and being lost.

It wasn't that there was too much wind, for the *drag* was no stronger than usual, and the kite hung there quietly and beautiful in the air, flapping its tail quite sedately. But suddenly it jerked madly and started coming down, slowly and headfirst, while Hannibal was left holding an empty reel.

We stood there horrified, watching the kite and seeing it twirl around itself and collapse and disappear far away over the dark waters.

"Well, I'll be damned. Have you ever seen anything like it? That's never happened to me before."

Hannibal is choking with disappointment and gloomy surprise: "The string was firmly fixed on to the reel. Or have you been fiddling with it?"

"No, I've not touched it."

Hannibal flung the empty reel away. Then he threw himself down in the withered grass and lay there for a moment on his stomach, writhing in sorrow and anger, and when he got up again, he stood for a long time wiping his eyes on his jersey sleeve.

"Oh, that *bitch*. There you see. That was getting her own back for the black cat. I ought to keep my mouth shut. And then you had to suffer for it, though you hadn't done anything, 'cos it was your kite of course. But she's such a disgusting person. She should... someone ought to throw a hymn book at her."

These words about the hymn book were something that Hannibal explained more fully as they made their sad way home.

It was Markus, the cooper in the Rømer Concern, who had once thrown a hymn book at Fina and hit her on the back of her head and knocked her out so she had to stay in bed for several days.

"Well, why did he do that?"

"'Cos she'd put a spell on his daughter."

"What do you mean, put a spell on her?"

"Well, she puts spells on women. She can do that as well."

Hannibal nods sombrely and refuses to say any more on that subject.

"But you shall have your ship back now, Amaldus."

"You don't need to."

"Well, then you shall have a new kite. A much bigger and better one. Just you wait."

***

When you had gone to bed that evening, you were excited to see whether the dead girl would come to you in your dreams, but you weren't particularly afraid, for it was probably only the Earth Girl Lonela and you weren't afraid of her.

She didn't come. But Fina the Hut came instead with her strange, big, dirty devil bird. She gave you a kind smile and had tears on her cheeks, and the bird hopped around clucking on one leg and with half unfolded wings that smelled like mouldy old clothing. And then you had to go into the Hut, and that wasn't nice because in addition to Fina and Dolly Rose there were both goats and crabs and some strange creature that was half horse and half man.

But then Hannibal came with his maroon, and everything disappeared in dust and smoke.

The Snilk

The Snilk lies rotting up in the grass.

The Snilk is a small, flat-bottomed dinghy. It's so rotten

that grass and pimpernel are growing up through its floor.

And it has been there since Ole Rilke drowned. That was ten years ago.

Ole Rilke drowned on his way out to a ship called the *Spurn*. It was a dark evening, and he was alone in the dinghy. The Snilk couldn't stand any kind of rough sea, and so it *capsized*.

Ole Rilke was only twenty-two when he drowned. He was studying to be a skipper. He was engaged to Anna Diana, Hannibal's mother.

No one knows for certain what Ole Rilke wanted on board the *Spurn* that evening. There are those who say they were having a binge on board.

Anna Diana (the woman who's your aunt – if that's true, for you can't always believe what Hannibal says) – Anna Diana later married Howler Hans, the crazy man who was Hannibal's father, and if Ole Rilke hadn't capsized with the Snilk, Hannibal would have been *his* son and not Howler Hans'. And then Hannibal would have been a quite different person from what he is now.

But what if Howler Hans hadn't married Anna Diana, but had a quite different wife?

Then Anna Diana would have married quite a different man, and *where would Hannibal be then?*

And if there hadn't been a do just that evening on the *Spurn*? And if Ole Rilke had rowed out there in a proper boat and not in the Snilk? And if the *Spurn* hadn't been in the roads just on that evening? And if the Snilk had never existed? And if your grandfather had never known Hannibal's grandmother?

If and if and if and if...!

But the Snilk exists.

The Snilk is still there, lying there gaping in the grass and doesn't know what it's done wrong.

There it lies, rotting, and it will soon be completely eaten up by damp and rot, and it will turn to earth and nothing.

Gale

It is autumn again, autumn – gales and surf and autumn, darkening skies and fleeing birds and flying leaves. Autumn, autumn.

The wind is coming in from the sea and it's cold and wet in the empty halls of the Castle.

When you lie on the floor in the Castle Hall and look out through the little peephole, you can see the waves foaming beneath the dark clouds. The wind blows in through your mouth and nose and tastes salty. The entire Castle shakes and trembles.

The Castle is called the *Sea Fort*. It's Hannibal's robber baron's castle. It is built of packing cases and stands on the sand down by the river mouth.

An old fisherman comes past; he cups his hands and shouts, "You can't stay here, lads, or you'll end in the waves."

"We know that, but we can't abandon our old Sea Fort now."

A huge wave comes and breaks and fills the castle's casements with water. If there are any prisoners down there they'll just have to drown.

A new wave, and now the castle starts to totter.

Again a huge wave, greenish and foaming, and now we can feel the castle beginning to float. So we have to jump ashore and stand watching the enemy destroy our splendid Sea Fort.

Then we grow angry. Angry and wanton like the hostile waves that are destroying our castle.

Then we have the dry, dark hour before the rain starts.

This is *Horn Time*. This is when Rydberg stands among the darkening trees in his dilapidated old garden behind the warehouses, when he stands there with his enormous green horn, stands beneath clacking trees, stands in a confusion of dry, brown leaves, stands in the brownish yellow sepulchral light of Horn Time with that fearful horn of his.

That's when you can hear the horn shriek and whinny through the roar of the surf, whinnying and snorting while we dance around high up here. While we dance and jump around in wild, senseless ecstasy in Ole Morske's sail loft, where hanging sails wave in the draft from the rattling peepholes.

"Who's Rydberg?"

Rydberg? Nobody knows. He died a long time ago. He used to live here in the warehouse and sleep in the bedroom up in the gable. Rydberg's a ghost, a man in the grave, a horn blower and storm blower; he blows rain and he blows night and darkness while we dance around and turn somersaults on the piles of canvas up here on the great empty floor in the greenish yellow stormy light at Horn Time. For Ole Morske isn't here, but he could come at any moment, and so we must hurry...!

And now it turns into a gale of the worst kind, and that is only a *good thing*.

Men shout to each other as they hurry to bring their fishing boats ashore and drag them up into the boat houses. Women with scarves flapping in the wind are going around looking for lost ducks and hens.

When it is lighting up time, the entire town is enveloped in an unbroken swirling mass of salt and foam from the sea; and then the lamps smoke in the wind and are blown out, and that is *good!*

Angry voices can be heard in the darkness, coming from up

on an old turf roof that the gale is trying to lift off and fly away with, and which some men are zealously trying to tie down and secure with ropes tied to big boulders.

The roof will probably blow off even so, and that'll do them *good*.

From out in the darkness there comes a sound as of hollow, plaintive cries for help. The entire town can hear this dreadful noise, which goes right through you. Some think it's the siren from a ship in difficulties. But we know that it is only the storm playing around in the old iron buoys out near the Bight.

Some people think it's the last trumpet sounding, and that'll do them *good*.

And then in the darkness we delight in the plaintive song from the sea and lie there full of dreadful, evil wishes. If only it would blow the church tower down! If only the sea would wash over the entire town so that all the houses went sailing!

The Feckless Idiots

Father no longer sails, but he has decided to work ashore and is now going to help Uncle Hans run the Rømer Concern, for it is "a colossus on feet of clay".

"What's 'a colossus on feet of clay'?"

Mother tries to explain that to you, but it isn't something that can be done in a jiffy; it takes time, for it's a "complicated story". But at any rate you gradually get some idea of it...

In your great-grandfather's day, the Rømer Concern was the biggest firm in the entire country. It owned thirty-two fishing sloops and two schooners carrying freight. And your grandfather, Amaldus Rømer, the one you are called after, could still more or less "keep it all together". But then he died, and his brother Prosper, "was never any good at anything but

74

sorting potatoes". As for your Uncle Hans (your mother's only brother) – "poor Hans", well there's no real go in him, no backbone although he will soon be twenty-five; he simply fools about and wastes his time together with his friends, Selimsen, Keil and Platen. They go off into the mountains on their horses, or they spend their time sailing around from one island to another in Uncle Hans' splendid new yacht, the *Nitouche*.

But now Father's coming, and he'll get the whole thing organised, for he's a captain and is used to being obeyed.

***

And so Father comes to get everything put right.

Father is big and strict, with stern eyes and a huge, weatherbeaten nose. And Uncle Hans and his friends are now no longer allowed to sit with their glasses of beer in the office, singing, "I've been born, so I'm going to live."

But then they still have the Factory.

The Factory is the biggest building in town, but it stands there empty as it "didn't pay", and the owner, who was a wealthy Scotsman, sold his Factory to the Rømer Concern and went back to Scotland. That was in Grandfather's day. Since then, the Factory has "lain fallow", but now Father is going to see about getting it going again.

For the time being, however, it is left empty.

However, one of its "halls" is often full of people – this is when Uncle Hans and his friends have their evening entertainments or dances out there, or when they put on a play.

Selimsen is an artist who wears a broad-brimmed hat and has an impressive moustache that turns up at the ends. Keil is a photographer who wears a frock coat and yellow skin gloves.

He's also known as the "Lieutenant", though Aunt Nanna says he's never been a lieutenant, only a *cadet* – the other title is only to show off, for he is a braggart. Mother calls him "a ladies' man", but Father has a more scornful term; he calls him a "gasbag".

Then there is Platen. Platen speaks Danish, but a curious sort of Danish, for he's a Swede. He is a fat, happy man with curly hair and a beard and a floppy tie, and he's musical and plays the cello, "and he plays it very well indeed", says Mother. He's really called *von Platen* and that's an aristocratic name. "And perhaps it's right enough that he's a baron," says Father. "But at all events, he's a *feckless idiot*. They're all *feckless idiots*."

"What's a *feckless idiot?*"

Father doesn't answer this, but sits there at the table sullen and brooding and refusing to answer anything you ask him. Aunt Nanna puts the tips of two fingers up to her lips; that means that you have to sit and be quiet when Father's eating and not disturb him in his thinking, for he has such a dreadful lot of things to see to.

***

There is a cellar window in the Factory that can't be closed, and through this window you can get into the huge, complex building with all its *halls*. In these halls, which all have walls made of rough old boulders from the mountains, there are high ceilings, but it is as dark in there as in a cellar, even in daytime, for the long rows of windows are right up at the top near the roof. It feels oppressive in here like in the Mountain King's castle. There are big basins and water pipes and strange machines in some of the halls, and others are full of empty crates and barrels, piles of crumpled lengths of tin and other rubbish, and then there's the boiler room where the tall steam engine stands and grows rusty. But some of the huge rooms are quite empty, so empty that even your stealthy footsteps produce an echo.

Then there's the Office. This is where you will find the big, dark green safe, which is so heavy that it has been impossible to move it, and in the corner there, standing in splendid isolation, is the huge Scottish fireplace, which is built of stone in various colours and is topped with a marbled slab. And along the walls there are fixed benches with leather covers. But there are patches of white mould on the fine dark carpet, and below the high windows overlooking the sea there is a half-dried pool of water.

Hannibal settles down comfortably with his legs up on one of the benches along the wall and lights a cigarette.

"Isn't it *good* here? This is where it all goes on."

"What goes on?"

"All that with our uncle and Selimsen and them."

"Who do you mean?"

"And the girls."

"What girls?"

Hannibal sits blowing smoke rings and looking up at the ceiling.

"No, I'm not going to say anything, 'cos I'm not going to gossip; I never do. Besides, our uncle's a nice man. And you're far too little to be told all those things. But I know all about it."

But then after all, Hannibal starts talking about this and that, though he uses such a strange, enigmatic language that it's really impossible to get much out of it. But it's all about Uncle Hans and his friends and various girls and women.

The Schooner – you know, that big, good-looking woman,

surely you know who I mean? Have you noticed how fat she's got?"

Here, Hannibal draws a big curve over his stomach.

"It's Selimsen that's blown her up. Girls can be blown up just like balloons. And then they burst one day. And then there's Dolly Rose; at least you know her. She's our uncle's. He's *got* her. He gives her both clothes and money. Oh, but now I've said too much already. 'Cos when all's said and done uncle's a nice person. But Dolly Rose's only sixteen. And I wonder what her mother, Fina the Hut, thinks about all that? Perhaps she's pleased? Perhaps she's put a spell on our uncle; that's what some people say at least. All I know is that if I'd been him I wouldn't have been so daft. I'd have kept my hands off Dolly Rose."

Hannibal has assumed his chieftain's mien and looks grown up and stern.

"And as for Keil, the photographer, he's a gutless twit, even if he's a hundred times a lieutenant. But he's got lots of them, I can tell you. He gets anyone he wants, 'cos they're all mad about him – and Aunt Nanna's one of them. As for Platen – no, he only comes here during the day, 'cos he's a much finer man than the others, even finer than our uncle, and almost even finer than your Father. For Platen's a baron. And then he's extremely well off. Yes, good Lord, he owns an entire *mine* in Sweden. But then he went on the bottle and so they sent him up here, 'cos they've said he can't look after his own affairs. But he never comes out into the Factory except to sit and play his cello. *Listen.*"

Hannibal gets up.

"He's there now. Come on."

The distant, deep sound is coming from inside one of the empty halls. Through the crack in a half-open door you can see

Platen sitting on a folding chair, bent over his cello and you can see his fingers on the fingerboard and the bow going to and fro. Then he turns a little to allow you a glimpse also of his beard and eyebrows as they catch the light from the windows up there and then his smiling features. He is sitting there with a delighted smile on his face as though he was together with someone with whom he was having an amusing, cosy chat. But he is quite alone.

"Why's he sitting there playing all on his own?"

"Because it sounds a lot better here than up in Mrs Midjord's little house where he lives. Can you see his bottle? He's always got to have it with him, otherwise he gets DTs."

"What's DTs?"

"It's something you die from."

Platen plays and plays, and the music comes in great waves from the reddish brown cello, as though full of subdued light and profound delight. You can feel the deep sounds right down inside you.

Platen is sitting here in the dark, clammy rock, smiling and enjoying himself all on his own.

He's a *feckless idiot*. They are all feckless. Good-for-nothings. Good-for-nothings.

***

You don't quite like Uncle Hans being called feckless, for you like him. Uncle Hans is always kind and good-tempered and he's always busy doing something amusing and exciting.

He takes you out sailing in his fine yacht the "Nitouche". Then he's a sailor with a shiny peaked cap or wearing a sou-wester. And when he's out riding in the mountains he wears riding breeches and leather gaiters. But when they are giving a concert out in the Factory and Uncle Hans stands *conducting* the "Ydun" girls' choir with his white baton, he is in "tails". Then they clap and Uncle Hans bows and smiles and points to the girls with his hand to show that the honour is theirs. And when they put on a comedy, there is no one like Uncle Hans to make people double up with laughter or weep with emotion.

But Father is angry with Uncle Hans and addresses some harsh words to him and he doesn't care whether others hear them as well:

"You'll never grow up! You think everything's a game. But the jar'll float on the water so long that it will come home without a handle."

Then Uncle Hans says nothing and makes no effort to defend himself, and he doesn't even look angry or hurt.

Later, when Father has gone, you hear Uncle Hans say to Mother, "I've really always liked the idea of this jar floating on the water instead of standing on the shelf filled with pickled gherkins."

***

But the biggest of all the feckless idiots is after all Uncle Prosper, who just stands by his duck pond and feeds his ducks.

There is a little brook that hurries through the garden at Andreasminde. It comes from somewhere up in the mountains and the great green grasslands. Once in the garden, it hides beneath the dense foliage of the redcurrant bushes, but it turns up again further down, and this is where Uncle Prosper has his duck pond.

Uncle Prosper's duck pond is divided off from the garden by means of a tall fence "so that we don't have to look at all that mess".

Uncle Prosper is Mother's uncle. He is quite small, indeed really not much more than a dwarf, but he has a big white handlebar moustache. He looks pretty strange in general, for he also wears smoke-coloured glasses and almost always goes around in sea boots.

Uncle Prosper has deep furrows across his brow like someone who has a lot to think about, but what he is thinking about is the duck pond and the ducks.

"It's a pity for Uncle Prosper. You must always be kind to him and not laugh at him."

Uncle Prosper has a "workshop" in the cellar of Andreasminde; here there is a table full of coloured pieces of paper and jars of paste, and on the wall there hangs a photograph of an old man with mutton chop whiskers; this is Uncle Prosper's father, "Old Rømer", who is your great grandfather. Old Rømer has fierce eyes, but still he looks as though he can't quite refrain from being secretly slightly amused at his impossible son Prosper.

Uncle Prosper loves to feed his ducks. He stands by the pond with his bag of bread and calls them each by name, for he has a name for each of them: Rabbirap and Rabbisnap, Big Malene, Old Malene and Little Malene, Andrik and Mandrik and Topperik and whatever. They come swimming along with their heads on one side looking at Uncle Prosper with one eye and curtseying politely.

Inside the wash cellar there is a big basin with running water, and swimming around here are Uncle Prosper's yellow ducklings that are not yet big enough to go out into the pond, where the big tomcat "Shitty Frederik" (that's the name Uncle Prosper gives to this fierce, predatory cat that can both swim and dive) goes around looking for an opportunity. Uncle Prosper is particularly fond of the ducklings; they are the apples of his eye, and he often stands and plays his little flower-decorated ocarina flute for them.

The eggs that Uncle Prosper's ducks lay are taken up into the kitchen and boiled or fried for him personally, for no one else likes duck eggs. But some of the eggs are "blown" and covered with coloured and golden strips of paper and tiny cut-out figures and hung up on the wall to be used as birthday presents and gifts.

When the weather is good in the evening, Uncle Prosper sits in a basket chair near the pond and smokes his long pipe. He will not be wearing his sea boots then, but will be in a dressing gown and skull cap and embroidered slippers as he sits and makes himself comfortable. Occasionally, he will leaf through an old picture book about Struwwelpeter and sit and chuckle through his beard and pipe smoke as he settles down in a seventh heaven.

***

Grandmother – is she feckless, too? Perhaps and perhaps not.

"Grandmother's so *naive*."

"What's naive?"

Mother hesitates for a moment over her ironing.

"Naive? It's when you think too well of everybody. And when you're too kind. And when you let others take advantage of you."

Mother and Aunt Nanna go on talking about how poor Grandmother has "let others take advantage of her throughout her life".

You sit there, half listening, while you are playing about with your schooner the *Christina*, whose name plate has come loose and needs to be fixed again with some glue you've borrowed from Uncle Prosper. A few strange words fix themselves in your mind, and you can't help wondering about them afterwards.

Your grandfather, whose name is the same as yours, *Amaldus*, – this grandfather was "a bit of a rake". And "dissolute". And a "toper". And poor Hans takes after him, unfortunately. And (here you prick up your ears) he was a "ladykiller" as well.

"Yes, he *was*, Nanna. He couldn't leave a skirt alone. And of course, Mother had no idea. She simply adored him. So did everyone else. Aye, 'cos he had a way with people. Everyone adored Father. Just as they do Hans now."

***

So Grandmother is *naive* (a lovely new word even if there is something rather sad about it) and she "lets everyone take advantage of her".

Grandmother is small, frail and very short-sighted, but when she sits at her piano and runs her small hands over the keys, it is simply wonderful to hear how she can make the big piano sound and how, through her glasses, she can work out all those countless black dots and curious forks and hairpins on the pages of the old music books. (In those days you didn't yet know that your Grandmother had had a strict musical upbringing in her native city of Copenhagen and that it was the original intention that she should have a "musical training".

Sometimes, usually on Saturday evenings, Uncle Hans and his friends come and make music together with Grandmother. And sometimes the Ferryman and his two sons come with their horn and violins and Platen with his cello. This is when they are to rehearse for an evening concert in the Factory. On such occasions, all kinds of people meet in the veranda room in Andreasminde. Pastor Evaldsen's male voice choir comes as well, and so does Uncle Hans' "Ydun" girls' choir to have their voices trained.

Then Grandmother is "really very much in demand", but she often becomes so tired that during the pauses she has to sit and *collapse* in her rocking chair and smell some invigorating scents from her "potpourri jar".

Then she sits and rocks a little and relaxes, but a moment later she is up again and with eyes radiant behind her glasses is once more a feckless idiot among the other feckless idiots.

Grandmother's toy theatre stands behind the round flap on the desk in the dining room at Andreasminde. It is her father's work. He was a horn player in the Royal Theatre in Copenhagen, and his delightfully painted and gilded toy theatre is "like the Royal Theatre right down to the least little detail". And the small coloured cardboard figures that are arranged on the stage are all well-known actors and actresses that Grandmother saw as a child and young girl and about whom she has so much to tell – "Mrs Heiberg", "Phister", "Anna Levinson", "Herold" and lots of others.

The toy theatre is a gem that no one is allowed to play with, but people are very welcome to look at it and listen to Grandmother telling what it is the tiny figures are doing. Sometimes it's an opera, and then Grandmother plays the piano and in a cracked but warm voice sings the "arias" and "recitatives".

Grandmother would most of all herself have liked to be a singer – but fate determined otherwise.

But (as Mother told me later, when Grandmother was long dead), one of the small figures on the stage of the toy theatre was *Grandmother herself.* And sometimes during the evening when she was playing with her figures she pretended to be an opera singer and would sing Cherubino's aria from *The Marriage of Figaro*.

But sometimes Grandmother sits all hunched up in her rocking chair and is so quiet and so far away in her thoughts that she looks almost like a cardboard figure. Then she mustn't be disturbed, but be allowed to sit and dream.

"What does Grandmother sit and dream about?"

"About Copenhagen and the royal palace and the King's Garden. And Kongens Nytorv and the Royal Theatre..."

The Little Singer

Then, one day it is Aunt Nanna's eighteenth birthday.

For a quite special reason, this day has been inscribed in your memory, so that you even remember the date: the 7th of April 1907. For that was the day when, for the first time, you found yourself in a room together with *Merrit*.

Aunt Nanna's birthday was on the same day as that of her sister Kaja, who was two years older than she. This double birthday, which was celebrated out in Andreasminde, was a particularly festive event; there were usually lots of guests, and they sang and danced and sometimes performed children's plays.

It was Grandmother's idea that little Merrit should come on that day and sing for the birthday guests. Grandmother gave piano lessons, and the eleven-year-old Merrit, the youngest daughter of a mate by the name of Svensson, who for some time had been Grandmother's pupil, had entranced her with her ear for music and especially for her singing voice.

And there you have Stare-Eyes, the girl from the church, standing by the piano and singing in a voice like the fine, white sand that runs through your fingers (that was how it seemed to you). She is wearing a pale blue dress and has a blue bow in her flowing hair and she isn't the least bit shy even though all eyes are turned towards her...

Nor have you forgotten what she sang, and you can easily name it even now: first there was an old romance from Grandmother's young days called *Rest in the Forest*, then Aladdin's lullaby by Heise and finally Cherubino's aria from *The Marriage of Figaro* (though only the first part). That was the star piece and it had to be performed twice. Then there was enthusiastic applause; Grandmother's eyes shone with delight and Uncle Hans came and lifted the little singer up and carried her into the dining room (where there were two birthday cakes on the table, each with a little dancer on top) and put her down in a place of honour alongside the two birthday girls.

"But she's an affected little thing even so," said Aunt Nanna later when we were at home again.

A Bright, Frosty Evening at New Year 1974 and I
(Amaldus the Ancient, the Survivor and the Reminiscer)
have just returned from a lonely voyage of discovery beneath the starry vault of heaven.

I took Father's ship's telescope with me, and the object of my excursion in the universe was to catch a glimpse of the comet about which they are writing and talking so much at the moment.

I couldn't capture it. But then there were so many other things to linger over in wonder and delight. All these twinkling eyes in the night that you got to know and love in your youth are familiar to you now as they were before and make you feel at home in the world. The steadfast seven lanterns of the Great Bear seen through a swirling foam of Northern Lights! Aye – it is still out there, that imperishable array, and the objective of its vast progress through Space is simply to greet you and delight your spirit by communicating to your perishable earthly Present an aura of eternity.

Those are your thoughts as, happy and excited, you sit there sharpening your pencil over the pages of your sketch book and shake the shavings down to join the ashes in your ashtray.

Happy and excited, yes indeed: and there are two reasons for that, for in our story we are now approaching a time of happiness that passes all understanding...

Ah, how am I to describe *that*?

One thing is certain, and that is that we are now in the middle of a great, scorching hot summer, surrounded by all its delicious scents and sounds. The perfume of grass and moss and all the plants in the field, the scent of bread and milk and peat smoke, stable and hay and washing that is hung out to dry in the evening air.

The sound of the curlews' warbling in the bright daylight and the deep dusk-like shawm of the snipe and the delicate notes from Grandmother's old piano!

And through it all: tremors of wild infatuation, a childish, dawning, still contained and shy Eros. But mighty indeed, mighty indeed.

For this whispering summer was entirely dominated by thoughts of *Merrit*.

The Life Bridge

Father and Mother are to go to Scotland on the *Christina,* and Aunt Nanna is going with them.

It is decided that you and Little Brother are to go and live at Andreasminde; then a girl called Jutta will come and look after Little Brother, for Grandmother hasn't time for that – she has to see to her piano and her pupils, and the two aunts Kaja and Mona can't neglect their jobs in the Rømer Concern.

***

Jutta lived close to Andreasminde, in a long, low, black-tarred house in the middle of green slopes with their profusion of waving grasses and nodding flowers, and in the midst of the whispering summer. Belonging to the house were a barn and some stalls in which the cows Star and Grima and the horse Jupiter were kept.

Jutta's father's grassland extended from the fence around Andreasminde right up to the great outfield fence at the foot of the mountains, where the heather took over. In this green and stony stretch of land there were hills and valleys and great rocks topped with blueberry and ling and there was a swift-flowing little stream along the banks of which you could lie in the grass and look up into the sky with its gently flowing clouds and lose yourself in its blue chasms and in the delighted gurgling of the mountain stream.

There was a bridge consisting of a single plank across this stream. You could balance your way over it as on a knife edge, so the bridge became known among folk as the "knife bridge". We, however, understood that as the "Life bridge" and as such it came to be known.

This Life Bridge still haunts my dreams to this day; indeed, even during wakeful hours I can lose myself at the thought of it and relive the prickling sensation it caused in me when I balanced my way across this narrow bridge with outstretched arms and "with my life in my hands". It was a bridge that led nowhere except to the other bank of the stream and which was of no earthly use, for without getting your shoes wet you could easily jump from one stone to the other in the little stream, and in any case you could wade across it.

But at all events, this bridge, this Life Bridge was *there*. Perhaps the plank was a spare one that had been in the way, and so it was put there: it wouldn't do any harm to have a bridge across the stream, which in point of fact could grow into a real river in rainy weather.

And how we loved that bridge and clung to it.

And we hung over it as well, lying on our stomachs and looking down into the clear, brownish yellow water in which tiny trout lay still with fins quivering, and where the midges danced above the mossy stones when the weather cleared up.

A certain tune has for ever been linked to the Life Bridge, a tiny piece in the minor key, a tune that for a brief moment modulates into the major and then back to the minor as when on a day of showers it stops raining for a moment and the sun shines and the midges dance.

The Life Bridge. There is some dark, strange, solemn symbolism associated with this name. "Now I'm crossing the Life Bridge – look, I'm flying." For it doesn't take long, no, one two three and then you are over and standing among the stones on the other bank. One two three – such is the brief span of life.

You didn't think like that in those days when you were still standing in the midst of a green eternity. But that's how you feel it now that you once and for all have crossed the Bridge of Life and – wonderingly – stand among the grey, lichen-covered boulders on the other bank, stand in this evening-shadowed land.

(And now perhaps I have written too much now about this poor, unimpressive plank but it is difficult to use but few words when it is a matter of reports from Paradise!)

Merrit

Jutta is twelve years old, but she is very big for her age, so big that I almost feel her to be grown up although she is only three years older than I. She has fair hair and small bright eyes, and her mouth is always slightly open, showing her big front teeth. She is always friendly and nice, but she doesn't say much, and when she does say something it's always a bit boring.

But then one day *Merrit* comes.

Aye, one day Merrit comes, and then everything is suddenly quite different...

Merrit is Jutta's friend and they are the same age, but Merrit is smaller and slighter, though her eyes are bigger than Jutta's. Merrit's eyes are not pale like Jutta's. Nor are they dark. They are green. Big, green, seeing eyes. For Merrit *sees* so much. And she knows a lot as well and can *do* so many things, and she also *says* such a lot.

"Early this morning, when *I* was the only one up, do you know what I saw? A huge rainbow. I was all on my own with it. It was so close I could touch it. Do you want to see a little bit of it that I caught? I've got it here in my hand."

Then she takes out a little square glass stopper and lets the sun shine through it, and see, she's got a bit of rainbow in her hand now.

"I can catch the sun as well."

She takes a bit of a mirror and holds it up in the light, and there you are: now there's a little sun dancing on her stomach and breast and neck and into her mouth so that it looks as

90

though she is swallowing it.

"And I can blow rain as well."

Then she blows into a hollow flower stem in which she has made a scratch with her finger. It makes a delicate whistling noise, but no rain comes.

"No, but it'll come soon. Look, the sky's already getting dark now."

And it starts raining before long.

Then Merrit sits there and lets it rain and doesn't mind getting wet, for it's her rain.

But then the shower passes and the sun, which is still high in the sky despite its being evening, shines on the wet grass, and the moss on the warm stones on the banks of the stream starts to steam. And the dun horse called Jupiter is standing out in the water.

Jupiter, our good friend, has worked faithfully throughout the day and is now standing out in the brook drinking for all he is worth, filling himself with water so that it rumbles and squelches in his belly. Then he slowly walks on to the bank and for a moment stands motionless on the greensward as though lost in deep thought.

But suddenly he turns over on his back and rolls in the grass, showing his long teeth in a whinnying grin. His huge, human-coloured, veined stomach wobbles, his shaggy pasterns wave at the heavens. Jupiter's good, gentle eyes have become mad and show the whites... what a sight, what a sight.

And Merrit's elbow in your side and her voice whispering in your ear:

"Can you see his thingummy?"

"His what?"

"His thingummy. That funny thing he's got between his back legs."

Yes, of course you can also see his thingummy just sticking out of the shaggy folds of skin.

But before long, Jupiter has got up and shaken off his frenzy and is grazing calmly and quietly as though nothing has happened.

But Merrit has more to tell you about the thingummy.

"Do you know what it's for?"

"Ye-es... of course I do."

"Yes, but it's not only for what you're thinking, 'cos if he sees a filly his thingummy gets all big and then he jumps on her. I saw it once somewhere else. And do you know what? The filly had a little foal, and it was so lovely, so lovely. Didn't you know it was like that? No, of course you didn't, Amaldus, 'cos there's such an awful lot you don't know. 'Cos do you know what you are, Amaldus? You really are so terribly stupid."

***

Such was Merrit, and at first you didn't really like her staring, green eyes, that not only could stare but also turn into long cracks full of laughter and mockery, and then there were her sharp elbows, with which she could give your ribs a friendly dig.

Little Brother didn't like Merrit either, and when she wanted to give him a kiss and a hug he cried out and fled across to Jutta. And even Jutta wasn't always too happy with her friend, for her eyes often took on a tired look when Merrit turned up, as though she wanted to say, "Well, now *she's* coming, so there's not going to be much peace any longer."

Aunt Nanna isn't keen on Merrit either, saying she's a tomboy and that she's terribly affected.

But Grandmother is very fond of Merrit because she is so musical and has "a beautiful voice" and "sings like a little angel".

Occasionally, you sit in Grandmother's sitting room and look through one of her picture books while Merrit's clever fingers play her scales on the piano, with Grandmother sitting beside her holding a pointer and wearing glasses. And when the lesson is over it happens that Grandmother will come with tea and buns, and then she will sometimes read a story to us from the book called "Fairy Tale Treasures".

One of these stories is about two fairies, a good one and a bad one; and you can't help thinking of Jutta as the good fairy and Merrit as the bad one.

The good fairy is fair-haired like Jutta and has gentle little eyes and big front teeth for which her mouth is slightly too small. The bad one has green eyes that sometimes are long and narrow and reflect some sort of vague amusement, and sometimes they are staring and not at all nice.

But one night you dream that the bad fairy has been caught and shut up in the dark coal cellar as a punishment for her evil deeds, and there she sits now, all on her own, staring out into the darkness with her big eyes and looking like both the Earth Girl Lonela and Merrit with the staring eyes.

Then you feel sorry for the bad fairy.

The Foal Girl

There are some lonely houses high up in the hills, and a big, dark man lives in one of them. This is Strong Didrik. Some people also call him Filly Didrik. He lives alone, and no one visits him.

Strong Didrik has been punished and was in the prison out in the Redoubt.

"What was he in prison for?"

Jutta doesn't know, or perhaps she won't give you a straight answer. But Merrit, who knows so much, also knows why Didrik had to be put behind bars out in the Redoubt.

"It was because he was a filly's boyfriend."

Jutta looks down and giggles and hides her face behind Little Brother's back. But Merrit's staring eyes are quite serious.

"It's nothing to laugh at. And do you know why he had to be punished, Amaldus? Well, because if Didrik's filly had a foal it would be a terrible monster. A troll! Well, what do you think trolls are then?"

"Oh, stop it, Merrit."

Jutta looks as though she is ashamed of her friend.

But Merrit doesn't stop; she knows a lot more about Strong Didrik and his filly. For when it was discovered that he was the filly's boyfriend and they came to take her from him, he got on the back of the filly and rode far off into the mountains, and there he let the filly loose so far away from people that no one could find her...

And Merrit knows still more.

"Come here, Amaldus, and I'll tell you something. Do you know what happened then?"

Jutta starts to hum.

"You're only trying to scare Amaldus, Merrit."

"No, 'cos Amaldus isn't at all scared, are you, Amaldus? If you are, I'll keep quiet about all the other things I know."

Jutta: "Yes, do, Merrit; that would be nice of you."

"Well, I won't even so. Just you listen, Amaldus – just imagine. Didrik's filly *did* have a foal up in the mountains, and she was a dreadful foal girl with a human body and a horse's head. And do you know what? She's still up there in the mountains, 'cos quite a lot of people have seen her and

94

heard her whinnying. And there are some who've seen her up at Didrik's house as well, 'cos she sometimes comes during the night to visit her father and to have some potatoes to eat, 'cos she loves potatoes."

***

That was what Merrit was like. And you could believe or not believe what she said.

But at any rate, Strong Didrik goes around heaping potatoes outside his house, big and gloomy, and he looks capable of anything. And one evening a curious frail and languishing whinnying was heard up in the hills. So perhaps it's a real horse, but it could also be Didrik's horse daughter who had come down from the fells to visit him and taste his potatoes.

The Cup Woman

And there are a lot of other strange people living out there in the green summer pastures.

One evening, the moon stands big and rust-coloured above the misty heather slopes behind the fence to the outfield.

The misty moon produces no shadows on the earth; it is simply there like a big, bare face in all the greyness.

"Look, Amaldus: here comes the Cup Woman."

The Cup Woman is on her way home bringing a load of peat from the heath. She is hurrying and hobbling along so that the peat bounces up and down in its basket, while the little blue cup she always carries with her is dangling from a woollen thread round her waist. That is why she is called the Cup Woman.

Merrit sits holding on to your arm as the Cup Woman

hobbles past with her basket of peat and her little blue cup.

The Cup Woman is very old, perhaps more than a hundred. She lives out in the Cup House, a tiny, overgrown stone hut right out by the gate to the outfield, where the heath begins. Here she lives with the Cup Man, who is her brother not her husband. The Cup Man is younger than the Cup Woman, but nevertheless so old that he has bumps on his head that look almost like horns. But he can still cut peat. And the Cup Woman is still so fit that she can help him to spread and dry the peat and stack it.

"And do you know why they stay so healthy even though they are so old? It's because they drink the water from a red iron spring up on the heath. When you drink the red water every day you can live to be over a hundred years old, 'cos it's a fountain of youth."

"But why doesn't everybody drink from that spring?"

Merrit has an answer to that question as well.

"Well, 'cos you don't only live to be old by drinking the red water – you also get so you can't remember anything. The Cup Woman and the Cup Man have forgotten everything. They don't remember where they come from or how old they are or what they're called. They only call each other *she* and *he*."

Ekka in the Well House

That was the Cup Woman. Then there is Ekka in the Well House.

Ekka is Jutta's aunt. She lives in an elegant, well kept house up in the hills and has her own field and keeps a cow and some poultry.

Ekka is always dressed in black, for she is a widow and wears mourning. She is mourning her late husband Bendik.

Ekka fetches water from a little pool in the stream that runs across her ground. It's a well made pool with stones around it; Bendik made it. It is called the Well, and so the house is known as the Well House.

Ekka brings her white bed clothes out into the field and spreads them out on the grass to get them properly bleached.

There is nothing strange about any of this. But now comes the strange thing, and again it comes from Merrit and is one of all those things she knows.

Well, during the night, when Ekka's bed clothes are spread out in the green grass, Bendik's lonely shadow comes and sees them lying there white and shining.

"What then, Merrit?"

"Well, Ekka knows perfectly well that Bendik is there, 'cos she can feel it in her bones. But what's the use if he's dead after all? Even so, Ekka wishes he would come in, even if he's dead."

"Does he come?"

"Yes. Just you listen. Dare you? Yes, 'cos it's really frightening. Just come and sit over here, Amaldus, 'cos otherwise even I daren't tell it."

It is a windy evening, all overcast; the wind soughs in the grass, and the water in Ekka's well is almost black with tiny curling waves. Merrit looks all staring.

"Well, you see, one day Ekka had taken her bed clothes indoors to iron them, but they had to be stretched first, and she couldn't do that on her own, but then she had the idea of fixing one end of a sheet to a door latch. And then, just as she starts stretching, there's Bendik suddenly standing in the doorway holding on the other end and helping her. *Amaldus!*"

"What's wrong?"

"Amaldus, I think he's here *now*."

"Who? Bendik?"

"Yes. 'Cos we've been talking about him so much."

And Merrit clings on to you, and you can feel her cold hair against your mouth. She's trembling with fear and daren't look up.

"Can you see anything, Amaldus?"

"See what?"

"Him."

"No, 'cos there's no one there."

"Yes, but he's there even so."

She gets up with a little scream.

"Come on."

And they rush off down through the fields.

***

But you can't get Ekka and her well house out of your mind again.

The candles on Grandmother's piano are lit during the gloaming. Then Merrit comes and plays *scales*. One scale is different from all the others; it goes right through you when you hear it.

"Why is it like that, Merrit?"

"Like what?"

You try to explain to her, but it's as though you don't quite know how to put it.

"No, but I know what you mean, 'cos it's right enough that it *is* like that. It's got its own name as well... what's it called?"

Grandmother knows. It's the "melodic minor scale".

The melodic minor scale is full of the dusk, and it makes you think of Ekka's well house and the well there reflecting the clouds in its dark waters. Then there are clouds and sorrow in the dark waters. And when Ekka's bed clothes lie out there shining in the grass as they are bleaching, Bendik comes and stands watching how the sheets and pillowcases turn pale and sad in the grass —

Then, one evening, the church bells ring.

"They are ringing for Ekka."

"Is Ekka dead?"

No, Ekka's not dead. They're her wedding bells that are ringing. Ekka has found a new husband.

And now there is no longer sorrow in Ekka's well; there is joy instead. And all the sheets and duvet covers and pillow cases in the bed where Ekka sleeps with her new husband are beautifully bleached and freshly ironed and full of joy and comfort.

But outside, beneath the sad night clouds, Bendik's pale shadow wanders about all alone.

The Big Sluggish Beast

That was Ekka in the Well House. But Merrit can tell about a lot more strange people and things and ghosts.

And then there's the worst of all: the Big Sluggish Beast.

"Have you never heard about *that* Amaldus?"

"No. What is it?"

Merrit looks as though it's something that isn't easy to explain.

"It's something that *creeps*. Do you know what it means to creep?"

"Yes, worms creep. And snails."

"Yes, but the Big Sluggish Beast isn't a worm, and it's not a snail either. But it *creeps*. It's always somewhere or other. Then it goes away for a time, but it comes back when you least expect it. *Creeping!* – No, perhaps it's best not to talk about it."

"Have you actually seen it, Merrit?"

"You bet I have."

"Well then, what did it look like?"

Merrit suddenly sits up and opens her stare eyes.

"Just listen here. It's slimy like a fish. And then it's got funny pink eyes that stick out. And then it cries and sighs and moans. 'Cos it's awfully sad. And then it comes and snuggles up to you. 'Cos it doesn't mean you any harm. It's simply so frightened and wants to be comforted. But it's so horrible that everyone runs away from it. And so it's all lonely and that's a pity for it. All you can do is say a prayer and say, 'Dear God, have pity on the Big Sluggish Beast and don't let it be so upset. And don't let it strangle me or suffocate me. Amen.' "

Merrit has tears in her eyes, and you yourself are almost on the verge of tears because you are so touched about the poor horrible and lonely beast.

But suddenly you feel her sharp elbow in your side:

"Amaldus. You really are so terribly stupid!"

The Churchyard

The wind hurries, the clouds hurry, the brook hurries, the soughing summer hurries, and it will soon be past, and then autumn will come.

In the great grassland, the grass is no longer green, but there it stands in flower with reddish violet wisps at the top. The haymaking has started; Jutta's father and uncle are out with their scythes, while Jutta's mother and some other women and girls spread the hay and then, when evening comes, rake it together into small stacks. And there it stands, looking like some big dwarf city.

Jutta and Merrit help with the haymaking as well.

But then, one day, Merrit is on her own in a corner among the stones by the brook, making a wreath of dandelions and stinking mayweed and other late summer flowers. It is to be put on her sister's grave, for it is this sister's fifteenth birthday today.

"What was your sister called, Merrit?"

"She was called Merrit – the same as me. She died before I was born, and so I was given her name. Mother says I'm like her as well. And perhaps I *am* her."

"Oh no, how could you be her, Merrit?"

"Well, perhaps her soul went over into my soul. And then, do you know what? That means I'm dead and buried even if I'm standing here as well."

"That means you're two people then. Is that possible?"

"Yes, it's possible. There are lots of people who are two people. Just think of all the women going around with babies in their stomachs."

Merrit's voice sounds so cheerful and she looks radiantly happy, although she is not smiling, for you mustn't smile in the churchyard.

"See, we'll put the wreath here. Now please, Amaldus, wait a moment while I say the Our Father."

Merrit kneels by the grave and sits there with her hands together and her head bowed. A few bedraggled cornflowers can still be seen in the grass. It's a dark, blustery day and it looks like rain. The wind blows over graves and crosses as though with brooms and dusters at the height of the spring cleaning.

Then Merrit has finished her prayer. She gets up and makes the sign of the cross over the grave.

"Rest in peace, Merrit dear."

It makes you shudder in some strange way to hear her say her own name over the grave, for suppose it was she, the live Merrit, who lay there dead in the ground. Horror and sympathy go through your mind in hot and cold waves; you want to take her hand and say her name, or simply to touch her a little and feel that she's still alive.

Then we slowly go out of the churchyard, looking at graves and gravestones on the way. Lovely white crushed shells have been strewn on the narrow paths between the Window Man's seven little grass-edged graves; the wind is whispering in them, and each of the graves has its own little wooden cross.

"And can you see the angel on watchmaker Girlseye's grave, Amaldus? She can't fly, because you can't fly when you've got stone wings. That's why she looks so miserable. Don't you think she looks terribly miserable?"

"Yes. But why was he called that?"

"Watchmaker Girlseye? Well, that wasn't his real name, of course. But that's what everybody called him. Perhaps because he had beautiful eyes. Or perhaps because he was one for the girls... Oh, God forgive me for what I'm saying; you mustn't say that kind of thing here in God's garden."

There is an enormous hawthorn bush standing on an almost obliterated grave. It's so bent and twisted that it seems to be writhing in despair. Merrit hurries past it as though she is afraid it might catch her in its claws.

At the gate, she makes the sign of the cross again.

"Rest in peace."

And then we are outside the churchyard.

"Do you know who's buried under that funny-shaped bush, Amaldus?"

"Yes. A suicide (everybody knows that)."

102

"Yes, and do you know what he was called?"

"No?"

"*Snorky*. A dreadful name, isn't it? And do you know what else? Come on, we'll go into Grandmother's garden and I'll tell you more about Snorky."

We go in and sit down on a bench in the open summerhouse in the corner of the garden. It's cold and draughty here. But from inside Grandmother's house there comes the sound of warm, scurrying notes on the piano.

Then Merrit tells about Snorky, the suicide. It's a nasty story about evil people, so it's a good thing that Grandmother is playing such a cheerful tune.

For suicides don't go to heaven, and so they have to stay on earth and be ghosts until Judgement Day. And Snorky has to live under his bush in the churchyard. So during the summer you can see his eyes deep down in the darkness behind the branches of the hawthorn bush. But in winter he has to hide in the ground with all the black beetles and worms and centipedes.

"Dare you listen to some more? No, it isn't all that dreadful after all, 'cos it all happened ages ago. But just listen: 'cos when Snorky was dead and buried, he came back and was seen in the dark by his wife Emma. For Emma was a nasty piece of work and she had always refused to give Snorky decent food or wash his clothes, and she used to biff him on the head with a broom handle when he was drunk."

"Did she kill him?"

"No, 'cos he did that himself. But do you know how he showed himself to her? Like a big black spider. And when Emma saw this big spider run across the kitchen table, well, bang! She stabbed it with the bread knife. And then there was a scream in the broom cupboard."

"Why was there a scream in there?"

"'Cos that was the cupboard he hung himself in. And then there were splashes of blood on the cupboard floor."

"Then what, Merrit?"

"Then Emma came with a cloth and wiped the blood up. And then she flung the cloth in the fire. And then she said something."

"What did she say?"

"No, I daren't say it now. Perhaps another time. *Amaldus*."

"Yes?"

"Amaldus, you'll have to take me home, 'cos I daren't go past the churchyard on my own. Come on. And you'll have to hold my hand."

"Yes, but that looks so peculiar."

"Yes, but then we must run. But make sure you run alongside me."

So we run and don't stop before we are outside the door of Svensson's house. There we stop and puff and catch our breath.

"Now I can tell you what Emma said when she threw the cloth with blood into the fire. Dare you listen? Come on, and I'll whisper it in your ear."

Then you felt her mouth against your ear and heard her voice as she whispered:

> Vanish like smoke in the earth below
> Melt like wax before fire and glow
> Vanish into fire and flame
> And never again let me hear your name.

The Kiss

Merrit *knows* much, much more.

But then there came a time when she didn't say so much herself, but sat rather and listened when you talked about some of all the things that you yourself knew.

And then there are a lot of things you both know.

Merrit knows the Ferryman, who sits blowing a horn outside his house in the evening when the weather is good. And she knows everything about the Wise Virgins. And she also knows Fina the Hut, but she doesn't know anything at all about the big black bird that comes and visits her during the night. And neither does Merrit know anything about the Old Poet's barrel of bones.

"Ugh, is that right? Have you yourself seen that there are dead bones in it?"

"Yes, and there's a dead girl's skull, and Hannibal wanted me to kiss it."

"Ugh, Amaldus. Surely you didn't?"

Then you tell her how the Old Poet came and took the head and put it in his barrel, and about Hannibal's robbers' den in the warehouse cellar out near the Bight, where there's the *maroon* that could blow up the entire building if you put a match to the touch paper. And Merrit shudders and has big staring eyes and sits gripping your arm.

Then you are secretly glad and proud that you have made her shudder.

And one evening you also tell her about the Earth Girl Lonela, the girl who sometimes comes to you in dreams and floats off with you.

Merrit listens with open mouth and big staring eyes.

"And what then, Amaldus? Where do you fly off to?"

"No, we just float."

"And does she kiss you then? Or do you kiss her?"

"No, why?"

"Well, after all, when you're out *floating* together."

"Well, she's *dead*, you know."

"Oh, of course, Amaldus. But suppose she was alive?"

"Well, what then?"

"Well, wouldn't you want to kiss her then?"

"I don't know..."

"No, 'cos you've no idea how to, have you? Come here and I'll show you."

And then you feel her cold arm round your neck and her warm breath on your face and her lips, which are neither warm nor cold, but feel alive and a bit sticky and just a little bit nasty, like when you touch an earthworm.

"Well, hug me a bit, Amaldus. You've got to hug as well. Yes, like that."

Merrit makes her voice deep and hollow:

"Now we're floating... Whoo–oo. Now you're out floating together with your *Earth Girl*."

Then her hand comes and ruffles your hair.

"Was it all that bad? Have you never kissed a girl before? No, I don't think you have, for do you know what you are? You're a *funny little puppikins*."

Then you think a little about this curious expression, which probably doesn't mean anything good, but perhaps nothing bad either, for her voice is warm, and she is nudging you in a nice way.

And yet, that bit about *puppy* worries you a bit, for the fact is that she is two or three years older than you.

***

But puppy or no puppy, the first kiss has come into your life now, and something has started that will never cease, something that brings great disorder and change in its wake so that nothing is as before.

And still today, a generation later, you can clearly remember both time and place for this event, an event that was both so tiny and so great.

That was just near the stream under the Life Bridge, and it was a Saturday evening. For when you got home to Andreasminde, Little Brother was in his bath being washed and scrubbed by Jutta, and in the living room Grandmother was rehearsing a song with Pastor Evaldsen's male voice choir ("Rejoice ye now, all Christian men").

And when you had gone to bed that evening you could see the evening star low on the horizon in the west, motionless and un-twinkling like a little moon... while you lay there and wished that the Earth Girl Lonela would come and fetch you out on a long, long floating trip, but she should be in the shape of Merrit.

The Willow Grove

High up in the hills, in an out-of-the-way place near the old, grey outfield fence, where the green summer land ends, there stood some weather-beaten dwarf willows in the midst of a motley array of wild grass and big, juicy sorrel. You could lie here out of sight and all on your own and as it were outside everything.

You used to lie in the grass here and long for Merrit when she was away.

It was not often she was away, usually only a few hours a

day, but once for several days on end, for her mother had been taken ill and so she had to "look after the house".

The memory of the infinite length of these days and the sense of longing is still in your mind like a deep sense of loss, and your inner ear can still hear the wind whispering in the grass and leaves of the Willow Grove – a sound that like the melodic minor scale bears a quiet complaint within it, but also something else, something joyful beyond comprehension: the first enormous, uncontainable, restless joy of falling in love for the first time – the feeling that no word can express, but for which music has always been able to find a happy expression in its wordless outpourings.

The Calf

Now the hay is in and the autumn gales are howling through the open hatches and doors in Jutta's father's barn.

Then comes the strange, empty time when the hayfields lie there desolate in the form of fields of stubble, the time when the last migratory birds have left and stars and Northern Lights again begin to be seen in the dark evening sky.

So *that* summer is past...

And one day the Life Bridge has gone, too, for Jutta's father has finally discovered what the excellent plank can be used for: a lamp post! The lamp is to be put up down by the gate in the fence out to the road so that the path up to the house, which has been far too dark otherwise, can be lit up in the evening.

So the "Life Bridge" is transformed into the "Life Light" as we naturally called this paraffin lamp as it cast a reddish glow over the pale wooden gate and the lichen-covered boulders forming the wall.

***

Then one day, Grima the cow has had a calf, and Merrit is quite crazy about the little baby cow that Grima lies licking and looking after while grunting tenderly through her nose.

Merrit almost has tears in her eyes.

"Oh, just see how she's lying there *singing* for her little boy."

"Why a *boy*, Merrit?"

"Well, it's a bull calf; you can see that because he's got a thingummijig. And then he's got a white star on his forehead, and that a sign of good luck. And what do you think he should be called? Daisy Star? No, that's a girl's name. What about Bobstar? Or Bigstar? Oh, just see how he's sucking his mother. Oh, he's so thirsty."

Jutta: "Yes, but he's only going to do that today and tomorrow."

"What then?"

"Then he's going to be slaughtered."

"Slaughtered."

"Yes, 'cos otherwise he's going to drink all Grima's milk."

Merrit looks somewhat crestfallen and isn't at all pleased any longer. Her stare eyes simply radiate disgust.

"Is he going to be *eaten* as well?"

Jutta nods.

"But then, what about Grima? What does she say to having her baby taken away from her and *killed*? Isn't she going to be simply furious?"

"No, 'cos she'll soon forget."

Merrit turns away.

"If I were Grima, I'd gore your Father to death if he came

to kill my baby. I'd get him on my horns and throw him right away, and that'd serve him right. Ugh, you are horrid, the lot of you."

And suddenly, Merrit goes off and slams the stable door.

Jutta shakes her head like a grown up.

"What a thing to go on about! And what a thing to say. Gore Father to death!"

Jutta is on the point of tears, and there is a little froth around her big front teeth.

"But do you know what Merrit is, Amaldus? She's a really dangerous little witch. That's what Father says, too, and it's *true*. Do you know what she did once? She set her hair on fire! What do you make of that?"

"Well why did she do it?"

"Because her mother had smacked her. And she'd really deserved all the smacks she got. But that's what she's like. And I'll guarantee she creates a lot of problems for her mother and father. And now she's going around sulking and upset 'cos the calf's going to be slaughtered. What a lot of rubbish."

"Where do you think she's gone?"

"I don't know and I don't care. Just let her stay away. But she's probably sitting around watching somewhere or other and thinking of something nasty to do, like setting fire to the house. No, you never know..."

***

But Merrit isn't to be seen anywhere.

It's a raw, windy day; big crows are hopping around on the fields of stubble and filling the air with their hoarse cries. Up by the stream, in the place where the bridge used to be, there are pale marks left by the ends of the plank where they have been placed on the grass. And up in the Willow Grove the wind-blown willows are turning yellow, and there are black snails eating holes in the few sorrels that are left.

And suddenly you are overcome by a vast sense of grief, an endless feeling of sorrow that the Life Bridge has gone – and that Grima's calf is to be killed – and that Merrit has wanted to set fire to herself. And that it will soon be winter and dark nights and perhaps the End of the World and Judgement Day as well, the day that comes when you least expect it, "like a thief in the night"...

And as you are on your own, you can just as well abandon yourself to your misery and allow free rein to your tears.

You threw yourself down in the wet grass, quite overwhelmed, with your face buried in the sleeves of your jersey and lay and surrendered to wordless distress.

But in the midst of your despair it was as though you saw a light, something like the glow from a lamp deep down in the darkness, or a lighthouse far out to sea, or a rising moon, and you whispered down in your wet jersey sleeve:

"Merrit, Merrit."

***

Then a long time passes without Merrit.

You certainly catch sight of her now and then, but it is as though she no longer sees you. Or perhaps she sees you, but doesn't really notice you, even when you meet and talk to each other.

She has other things on her mind. You still have hardly anything but her.

And the more distant she grows from you, the more you have to think about her and long for her to come back and be as she was before as on that occasion by the stream under the Life Bridge in the great, green, soughing summer.

The Concert

Grandmother and Merrit are planning something together, something very exciting. They play and sing every afternoon out in Andreasminde, practising and practising, so much so that Aunt Kaja has a headache and has to go around with cotton wool in her ears.

"It's a pity for that girl that Mother bosses her about like this. Now the poor little thing's being turned into an infant prodigy and concert singer, 'cos she's 'a future Jenny Lind' now."

The concert is to be given out in the Factory. The money it earns is to go to the Cup Woman and the Cup Man, the two of them being old but unable to die and not having anything to live on either.

It is not only Merrit who is to sing; Uncle Hans and the Ydun girls' choir are going to as well, and Pastor Evaldsen's male voice chorus. And there is going to be an "orchestra" and "tableaux" and other exciting things. And Grandmother is going to contribute to it all with her piano, so she has plenty to see to at this time.

But even so, Grandmother is in her element.

"If all goes well, this will be the best evening's entertainment we've had up here yet."

One of the halls in the Factory is decorated with flags and streamers. A platform has been built at the end of the hall, and Grandmother's old piano is fetched and lifted up on to it. That makes it go out of tune and it has to be retuned, but the Ferryman can do that because he's got "such a wonderful ear".

Merrit is standing at the entrance to the Andreasminde garden, holding her music case.

"Aren't you dreadfully excited, Merrit?"

She looks at you with cold eyes as though she doesn't really understand you.

"Excited? Oh, you're thinking of the concert. No-o. I'm used to all this by now. I suppose you'll be coming to hear us, Amaldus?"

No, Merrit is so strangely aloof and so grown up that you feel endlessly little and foolish.

Then suddenly she smiles and there comes a warm look in her eyes.

"Come here, Amaldus, I want to whisper something to you."

Then you feel her mouth and her breath against your ear.

"I'm *terribly* afraid. And I'm upset as well. 'Cos do you know what: your Aunt Kaja says that I've got a voice like a tin whistle!"

"What's a tin whistle?"

"It's one of those like your Uncle Prosper plays for his ducks, you know, the little round one with flowers on."

Then you want to say something to console her, but it is not so easy.

"Well, Merrit, you don't need to take any notice of that."

"No, 'cos Kaja's simply envious. And do you know what Lieutenant Keil says? He says I sing like a lark."

"Well, so you do, Merrit."

Then Merrit gives a little wave like a grown up and is again a stranger, a bird of passage.

***

In one of Grandmother's hidey-holes in the upper loft in Andreasminde, I (Amaldus the Reliver and Relater) recently (while searching for something quite different) found a large, faded poster containing the entire programme from that concert in which Merrit made her public debut. The charming poster was done (in elegant black lettering) by Selimsen the artist, while a whole herbarium of flowers had been pasted on to decorate it.

The programme is reproduced below, along with Grandmother's pencilled notes on who each performer was here in parenthesis:

1. Prologue.
(Bergh, the headmaster.)

2. Arise all things that God hath made, traditional melody. Denmark, Denmark, sacred sound, Weyse. Swedish folk song melody.
(Male voice chorus.)

3. *The Princess sat in her Maiden's Bower,* H. Kierulf. Before your foot I bow down deep. Tenor soloists with humming voices.
(Hans.)

4. Intermezzo from *Cavalleria Rusticana,* Mascagni. Horn and piano.
(The Ferryman.)

5. Comedy Overture No. 1: Keler Béla. Salon orchestra.
(Violin and viola: The Ferryman's two sons. Flute: Olsen, the

114

bookbinder. Cello: Platen. Horn: The Ferryman. Drums and castanets: Bærentsen the victualler.)

6.   Folo Fola Blakken, Edvard Grieg. Aladdin's Lullaby; Heise. Soprano solos.
    (Merrit.)

7.   Tableau I: Saul and David.
    (Mr. Bergh and Lieutenant Keil)

8.   Tableau II: Stanley meets Livingstone in Africa.
(Selimsen and Degn, the bookkeeper.)

9.   Tableau III: The Girls from Southern Jutland.
    (The Judge's two daughters, Minna and Jenny.)

10. *Androcles and the Lion,* Drachmann. Recitation.
    (Pastor Evaldsen.)

11. Cherubino's aria from *The Marriage of Figaro,* Mozart. Soprano solo.
    (Merrit, undoubtedly the high spot of the evening.)

12. Eighteen juggling and disappearance tricks.
    (Keil.)

13. Hush, friends, Bacchus is sleeping, Bellman. Canon: My stomach is giving me terrible pain, Weyse.
    (Ydun Girls Choir.)

14. *May peace now dwell o'er town and land,* Weyse
    (Mixed choir.)

And, while we are at it: Grandmother's comments written on the back of the programme:

Oh, Heavens above, we've done it now. And it all went quite well, and some of it was really quite good even though (as always) there was something wrong with almost everything, a couple of times quite disconcerting, but never entirely scandalous.

Hans was a little too emotional in his singing (unfortunately, he had quite obviously already had a drop to drink!) and the humming voices were too loud. As always, the Ferryman played his horn splendidly. The comedy overture, heaven help us, was only so-so and far too loud and a little uneven, and then, naturally (!) it happened that Platen, who is such a heavy person, had a chair that was far too rickety for him and he broke it when he sat on it and fell slowly over backwards, holding his cello, to the accompaniment of a dreadful sound of splintering wood. But, thank God, Keil and the Ferryman caught hold of him so that neither he nor his instrument came to any harm. But it caused quite a disturbance, and there was a certain amount of justified laughter in the hall, and then we had to do it all over again from the beginning.

The tableaux were elegantly arranged by Selimsen, but here, too, things went wrong, for King Saul, played by the headmaster, whose noble shape otherwise suited the figure so well, had a fit of sneezing; that naturally gave rise to laughter, and Bergh ought to have taken that in good part instead of sitting there glaring at the audience and looking hurt. But Stanley and Livingstone were both good, indeed almost perfect, and the jungle setting and the "natives" (people from the warehouse and the Rømer Concern) were very convincing! And the Judge's daughters were charming as "The Girls from Southern

116

Jutland", and Pastor Evaldsen's reading was really moving.

But the best was undoubtedly my little Merrit. A lot of handkerchiefs were taken out as she sang *Aladdin's Lullaby*, and just imagine: in Cherubino's aria she managed all the modulations without blinking; it only went wrong once (the low D towards the end was dead).

There was a great deal of applause and enthusiasm. After the concert, Pastor Evaldsen came and shook hands with us (and also with Merrit's parents) and said that Merrit was a girl of whose ear for music we could expect great things. I was so pleased for them. And then there was the most beautiful gift for Merrit; it came from Platen – a gold ring with an emerald set in it, just think, a genuine emerald!

Afterwards, there was a reception at which punch was available for all, but I had to go to bed early, for I was dead tired.

***

As I sit now making copies of these comments by Grand-mother, I can clearly recall the scent of *incense* that filled the big, rather chilly factory hall in which this unforgettable entertainment took place.

This incense was an idea that came from Selimsen, the artist; it was intended to drown the persistent smell of discarded fish and train oil that filled this magic castle, a relic from its former time as a factory for the production of fish balls. To achieve this, some incense burners had been established, that is to say barrels and casks decorated with coloured paper and filled with heather and dried moss, bitter orange peel, bay leaves and other things that could be burned to produce a singular smell that many people found unpleasant and disturbing, but which we children thought great fun. And when at the same time I recall the music, I have it all before me as vividly as can be wished: the stage decorated with flags, those taking part all dressed in their Sunday best, the gentlemen with starched collars, messrs Berg and Degn even in dress coat and morning coat respectively, Grandmother in an old-fashioned but not unbecoming get-up with a sort of modest bustle.

But dominating it all there was Merrit, in a white summer dress (also in a rather old-fashioned cut, probably found in Grandmother's wardrobe), with blue ribbons in her hair and a somewhat shy smile in her big stare eyes... and the thrill that went down my back when the voice I knew so well was heard in song and so became something quite *different*, something that was not addressed only to me or to Jutta or Little Brother, but, all those people who were listening attentively and open-mouthed, a whole audience of strangers, indeed the entire town.

It was a transformation like the one that took place with Hannibal's kite when it got away from the earth and hung up there high in the clouds playing its remarkable celestial game in the blue of the sky...

***

I was allowed to see Merrit's diamond ring the very next day when I came across her in the garden at Andreasminde. The green stone looked like an eye, it didn't glitter, but there was a deep, sleepy glow to it, as if it were coming from far away or deep down.

"And do you know what Platen said? He said it was an old ring to bring you good luck and grant you a wish, but that you can only make one wish in your life so you have to wait before making it."

"Well, in that case you'll have to wait."

"Yes, and I'm going to as well. Have you ever seen a precious stone before, Amaldus?"

"No."

"Well then, you've seen one now. Oh, but I've got to hurry."

And she did her grown-up wave and disappeared through the garden gate.

When, Last Night, I, Amaldus the Aged, put out my Writing Lamp at about Two O'Clock

there was just a clear, starry pause in the everlasting rain and sleet of this January, and the sight of Sirius, low over the sea, wonderfully sparkling and huge, put me into a state of ecstasy as it had so often done before.

This, the diamond-like nocturnal sun of the ocean, which sends us its vital greeting from distant times and Space: all the colours of the spectrum reside in its ecstatic glints, from the coldest icy green to the most intense red, the red of a drop of blood, and if the weather is calm, as it was last night, it reflects its radiance in the ocean's waves.

***

Star and eye do not share the same time, but they have their secret meeting place beyond time, and never did mortal eye have a more splendid gift than the light from Sirius, this star of all stars.

The Lunar Eclipse

Then came the winter that will always be fixed in my memory as "the winter with the lunar eclipse".

Short, dark days. Well, they weren't really all dark, indeed the odd one was even so bright that the venetian blinds had to be lowered in the classroom where Miss Gudelund was taking her lessons in "general knowledge" so that she shouldn't have the sun right in her eyes when sitting at her desk.

In Miss Gudelund's general knowledge lessons we had so far only learned about life in the distant country called Denmark from which she came – about the villages with their churches and village ponds, about the forests with their beech trees and birdsong, about Kronborg Castle and other splendid old castles, and about Copenhagen with its towers and spires, all shown on big paper rolls that could be unfolded on the wall. But one day there was a *globe* on Miss Gudelund's desk, a most magnificent toy, a wonderful thing to see. There was a gasp of delight and surprise throughout the classroom when the teacher gave the globe a push so that it turned round on its stand like a top. She allowed it to whirl around until it stopped of its own accord. Then she spoke words that were mysterious and which I have never since forgotten:

"Well, children, what you can see here is the Earth, the planet on which we live."

We had naturally already heard something about the world being round, though without really attaching much significance to it, but now we could see it before our eyes: the Earth is round and it floats in an enormous circle round the Sun, which is also round, but much, much bigger, as much bigger than the Earth as an orange is bigger than a pea.

Yes, these were mighty words, historical words; but we

small denizens of the Earth thought at first that it was only a joke, for the teacher was a cheerful and rather mischievous lady who liked to shake us out of our inattentiveness by means of droll and surprising remarks. But then we could usually see a twinkle in her eye, and there was no twinkle today.

She gave the globe another push and made it turn, but more slowly this time. Then she went on in a gentle, calm voice:

"You see this is how it turns as it travels round the Sun, and we are with it on that journey, including you, Amaldus! Yes, including you, because I can see from the look on your face that you think I'm having you on. But if you don't believe the Earth is round you can go outside at eleven o'clock this evening and *see* that it is. Because this evening there is going to be a *lunar eclipse*."

Then our teacher goes on to explain what a lunar eclipse, an eclipse of the Moon, really is and she draws lines and rings on the blackboard, but in the midst of it all she becomes strangely tired and wipes it all out again.

"No, I can't expect you to understand any of this at your age, and in any case that doesn't matter. But you really should go out and see the eclipse if the sky's clear, as I think it will be and then you'll see something that happens only very rarely."

***

"Is the Earth round?"

Mother gives me an apprehensive and rather worried look.

"What are you asking that for, dear? Yes, of course the world is round. But I don't really know anything about that. Except that it was God who made it round when He created it. You'd better ask your Father."

Father nods and puts down his pen on the edge of the

inkwell. Then he pushes his chair back a little from the big writing desk and sits there for a moment, stretches and yawns. This means that he is in a good mood and is "relaxing".

"You want to know whether the Earth's round? Yes, it certainly is. And then it revolves around itself and that's why we have night and day. And then it goes in a ring around the Sun, and that's why we have the seasons."

Then he gives you a gentle smile and tugs your hair as though it was all just empty talk and some kind of a waggish idea.

"You look as though you simply don't believe that the Earth is round, Amaldus. But if the weather's good at about eleven o'clock this evening, you 'll be able to see how round it is for yourself, because we'll be able to see its shadow on the Moon! Look, let me show you how it works. Find something or other that's round, a ball or a ball of string."

"An orange?"

"Yes, an orange would be all right. And then this ashtray."

He puts the round, yellow ashtray on its edge and moves the lighted table lamp a little.

"See, the lamp's the Sun and the ashtray's the Moon, and then this orange can be the Earth. And now the Sun shines on the Moon and makes it light up. But here comes the Earth rolling along and casting its shadow on the Moon, like this, and you can see how round the shadow is. But perhaps we'll be able to see it all much better this evening."

Then Father puts the Sun back in its place and takes the Moon down from the sky, knocks his pipe out on its yellow surface and flicks the orange: "Just you peel the Earth and eat it, Amaldus, and then we'll be shot of *that* for a bit."

***

Then evening comes with a clear sky and a Moon that is red as it rises, just as it needs to be.

From the veranda steps at Andreasminde there is a good view of the open sky over the sea. There is still no shadow to be seen on the clear Moon that is reflected in waters that are alive with lines formed by the currents. It is Uncle Prosper's birthday, and in the dining room Aunt Nanna and her sisters have set the table with gilt-edged cups and a large yellow sponge cake. It was made with lots of duck-egg yolks, and the layer of meringue made from the whites is adorned with a host of apricot halves like little shiny moons. Uncle Prosper has arranged this himself. He is sitting in a rocking chair, puffing away cheerfully at his long pipe; he is enjoying himself and looking forward to the cake.

This lunar eclipse is taking its time.

Then Grandmother sits down at the piano, where the candles are flickering in the draught from the open veranda door, and plays a cheerful piece of music. (A rondo by Schubert – and when you recall it in your mind you still have a clear sense of this entire situation from more than half a century ago: the warm sitting room with the table set for chocolate, the tremendous cold shudder from the desolate moonlit heavens – and a huge and painful longing in your soul because the lighted candles on the piano make you think of Merrit!)

But now things are starting to *happen* up there in the sky.

Father stands out on the veranda steps with his big telescope to his eye.

"Now you can see some fun. The Earth's shadow's starting to eat the Moon now."

Aunt Nanna (cold and with teeth chattering): "Oh no."

Mother (wrapped in a light-coloured shawl): "Oh dear, yes.

I don't like it either."

You feel her arm on your shoulder. The homely smell of her woollen shawl is mixed with the cold breath of air from the sea. The Moon looks as though it would like to get away from the Earth's shadow, but it's too slow on the move, for the huge shadow has already settled on it.

Mother grasps your arm and shudders and doesn't like this shadow of the Earth; she can't bear the thought.

So we stand and watch it *happen* out there in the depths. It's a dreadful event, something like a *murder*. And yet it's nothing, simply a game in the air, like when Hannibal's kite plays its games in the sky. But far, far greater, so great that it leaves a heart-stopping sense of emptiness in your head and right down into your stomach and then on down into your feet as you stand there on a round Earth that is floating freely in the heavens...

Father's voice (which at this moment seems to you to be alien and full of some indeterminate horror):

"There you are, Amaldus, there's the proof that the Earth is round."

The moonlight has become strangely dark or grey, an ominous light settles on the stone steps and on all the faces peering up into the sky.

Then something more happens – something unexpected that also makes Father start and say, "Oh, just look now." For a long strip of light suddenly appears in the heavens, like some gigantic spear up in the sky that has been thrown from the stars to defend the Moon against the Earth's shadow...

Little Brother (standing there dancing, with a voice full of delight): "Look, it's *all* going off now."

Father: "That was *some* shooting star... wasn't it magnificent?"

Mother (sounding a little concerned): "Oh, is that *really* all it was? Well, in that case you can make a wish. *Wish* for something, Amaldus. Hurry."

Little Brother (hurries): "I wish for an elephant."

Father (roars with laughter): "An elephant. Well, why not?"

But then everything is silent again, an oppressed, anxious silence, while the sinister shadow of the Earth moves slowly but mercilessly forward – like a *fate*.

And there you stand, dizzy and horrified – but at the same time delighted, filled with a boundless sense of being out on the wildest of wild sledge rides, down steep mountain slopes and out over the edges of threatening abysses. Unease so enormous that it turns into ease, into a quiet, majestic sense of wellbeing beyond all understanding.

Mother (who can no longer stand the sight of this lunar massacre): "Can you see the *Pleiades,* Amaldus? And the *Milky Way* right at the top?"

Little Brother: "Why is it called the Milky Way? Is that where milk comes from?"

Mother: "No, it's called that because it's white like milk."

Father: "It's all lots of stars. Millions of planets and suns. Billions of them."

Mother (in a voice that is deeper than usual): "They are God's breath."

And now you are very curious to see what Father will say to *that*. Suppose he said, "Do you know, Else? You're just a *feckless idiot*." But he doesn't say anything, and Mother repeats in a voice that is strangely deep and emotional and almost threatening: "God's breath, yes. The Creator's mighty, mighty breath."

Uncle Prosper (standing puffing out blue clouds of smoke up into the heavens): "Let heaven look after its own problems, and we'll look after ours. The Moon's made of green cheese and the Sun's an Edam cheese. We knew that even as children; and we knew as well that the Earth's a bread roll. And it's all nothing more than our dear old Lord's supper."

***

Finally, the darkened face of the Moon is lit up again; a lovely bow of light emerged from the darkness, a new Moon that happily grew into a half Moon and finally into a round, dazzling and as it were full Moon all scrubbed clean and polished.

The Death of Platen

Thus the winter of the eclipse passed.

Then came, "the spring when everything became different".

Not everything, of course. The sun shines and the rain rains as usual; the sea glistens and sparkles; ships come and go. The wind howls in the gables and the fences out in Jutta's father's grassland, and the midges dance in freshening weather above the burbling brook. Yet nothing is, "as it used to be".

"As it used to be" and "long ago" had already entered your life. Once long ago, Merrit sat out in the rain in the green hills. Once long ago we balanced with outstretched arms across the Life Bridge. And long ago – and this really *is* long ago, for it was in the very beginning of time – there was a Tower at the furthermost Edge of the World. Now, there is no longer any furthermost Edge, for the World is round and there is no Edge to it. But instead of the mist-filled abyss, where God's Spirit used to hover over the waters, something even more overwhelming has appeared: the star-filled Space in which the Earth sails around the Sun, and the Moon around the Earth.

When the wind is blowing and the air is full of scurrying clouds, especially towards the evening, you can feel the Earth *sailing*.

On one such sailing evening, you met Merrit carrying her music case under her arm and on her way out to Andreasminde.

"Come with me, Amaldus. Then I'll play that piece you know. The *scale*, you know. Our scale."

"Oh, *that one*."

"Yes, and then afterwards you can take me home, 'cos do you know...?"

Merrit is wearing her stare eyes. She comes close to me and touches my hand, and I can feel her breath in my ear.

"Platen's terribly ill; he might die tonight."

We walk past Madame Midjord's little house, where Platen lives. There is a light in his bedroom window in the gable. You were up there once with a bag from Uncle Hans (a bag in which there was something that gurgled). Platen lay fully dressed on his bed, fat and heavy and slightly blue around his nose and with kindly eyes that stood out a little and had red veins in the whites. It was a very little room; its sloping walls were covered in flowery wallpaper, and his duvet cover was also flowered, and Platen winked merrily at you:

"That's lovely, my boy. You have your uncle's kind, bright eyes, and that's something you can be pleased about. Come on, you and I are going to have a little drink."

And he put two glasses on the table and poured something clear and thin into one of them and something red and thick in the other, and then he nudged you and said, "*Cheers*".

Merrit's elbow and shoulder against your arm, and her whispering voice: "Perhaps he's dying at this very moment. Your uncle and Selimsen are up with him to help him when he dies."

"What do you mean: help him?"

"Oh, just be with him and hold his hand."

Grandmother sits staring into the air and it seems her thoughts are far away.

"Aye, it's a pity about Platen. He's such a splendid man. But he's so weak, so weak."

The candles are lit on the piano, and Merrit's fingers hurry up and down the black and white steps of the scales while you sit looking through one of Grandmother's picture books without seeing the pictures. And the wind howls in the gable, and clouds filled with gloom scurry across the pale sky at dusk, and you have a salt taste in your throat from unspoken apprehension. Not emotion concerning Platen, but something else. This something else is Merrit, sitting there and playing "our" scale while Grandmother sits deep in thought with her eyes closed behind her glasses, sunk into reverie and far away in her thoughts...

When on our way home we passed Madame Midjord's house, quiet singing could be heard through the open gable window: "Am I born, then I will live."

Merrit stopped and listened.

"Then he's not dead yet. *Amaldus*."

"Yes?"

Then you feel her cold arm round your neck and her warm cheek against yours. But only for a moment, then she nudges you and pulls at your jersey.

"No. Come on. I've got to hurry."

***

You lay for a long time that night unable to sleep, thinking of what Platen had said on that occasion when you drank to each other and of the sweet taste in his raspberry juice. But that was not all that made you lie there clutching your pillow and making it damp and warm with your tears. That was something quite different. And that quite different thing was *her*.

And the tones of the melodic minor scale ran up and down their steps as you lay there and whispered her name down into your clammy pillow.

***

However, Platen did not die until some months later. He died on the longest day of the year. He died late in the morning, just as the schooner the *Christina* had arrived and dropped anchor in the roads and lay out there with its masts and its yards and its gilded figurehead, and the sun was shining at its brightest and all the Rømer grounds out near the Ring were white with drying fish.

He died while we boys were out playing Robin Hood and shooting our bows and arrows up in the fields near Ekka's well house.

Then Ekka came out of her house and stood peering down over the town.

"Can you boys tell me whether Rømer's flag is flying at full mast or half mast?"

"Half mast."

"Then Platen's dead."

Then we stopped playing because Platen was dead.

Erik August von Platen was the full name of the man who had now died. Ekka told this and that about him in a sad voice, on the verge of tears. He came from a fine, extremely wealthy family, but they had disowned him because he couldn't look after his money and frittered it away in his uncontrollable desire for drink, poor man. Then he came here on the *Christina* and settled down in Mrs Midjord's house, and Mrs Midjord earned a lot of money for taking care of him. He was drunk most of the time, but otherwise he was always nice and kind. But then he fell ill, and the doctor couldn't cure him of that illness for it was something to do with his bowels, which were entirely eaten up by all those glasses of strong schnapps. Then they sent for Fina the Hut, and she came with some herbal mixtures, and they were a help, but only for a time. Then you could see Platen sitting in his basket chair outside Mrs Midjord's house when the weather was good. There he sat, rocking his white walking stick and talking to folk passing by. Aye, he was always in a good mood. God rest his soul...

***

Later that day, Uncle Hans came and told us about Platen's last hours and sat there with tears running down his cheeks as he spoke. He had sung Platen to sleep, indeed, he had sung him into his last sleep. He had at last sung his favourite song, *'My life is a wave'*. Then Platen had said, "Goodbye, Hans. Now I'm going into my tapestry."

Those were his last words.

Aye, strange words. And the very moment his soul departed, Selimsen, who was on his way up towards Mrs Midjord's house, had seen a white mist floating above the roof of the house, a mist in the shape of a man with his arm raised.

Father: "Of course."

Mother: "What do you mean: of course, Johan?"

"Well, Selimsen had naturally *had a drop* to mark the day!"

***

130

Then Mrs Midjord came; she was wearing a mantilla of black spangles and smelled of lavender and it was quite obvious she had been drinking rum, and she wept a great deal and held Uncle Hans' hand.

"He was as good as the day is long, was Platen. He had such a gentle nature."

Mrs Midjord unwraps something from an embroidered handkerchief. It is a piece of jewellery, a gold ring set with a blue stone. She holds it up in the light so they can see how the stone shines.

"A real sapphire. He gave it to me."

Then we boys went down to the mouth of the river where Johan the carpenter was standing in the sunshine outside his workshop, planing wood for Platen's coffin. Here stood The Wise Virgins and Spanish Rikke and some other girls and married women talking to each other in plaintive voices.

"He was so kind and so charming, but so weak, so weak."

"He was a poor *soak.*"

"No, Rikke, you can't say that sort of thing now he's standing before God's throne."

***

That evening, a great many people had gathered in the garden of Andreasminde, sitting in the summer house with their glasses and remembering the dead man, and Uncle Hans and Selimsen sang, *"My life is a wave"*, and Selimsen went indoors to Grandmother and asked her to play a funeral march. (Grandmother played the one by Mendelssohn – and when the dark, agonising sounds came floating out of the open window, you had to hide yourself and your emotion in a flowering redcurrant bush.)

Then night fell, although the sun still shone on the red flakes of clouds high up in the air.

But on board the *Christina*, the sailors were playing the accordion, and you could hear there were girls on board and that they were dancing and fooling about even though Platen was dead.

Mother closed the window.

"That's something *you* ought to have been able to stop, Johan."

Father stood with his thumbs in his waistcoat armholes and with an extinguished pipe between his teeth.

"There's no reason to be so miserable just because the poor feckless idiot has finally got what he wanted."

"What do you mean by *wanted*, Johan?"

"Well, drinking himself to death. But let's hope it can be a lesson for that crazy brother of yours."

Then you glance at Mother and see the pain in her eyes and feel a wave of sympathy of which you are also a little ashamed of at the same time.

Cadenza in the Willow Grove

Platen was buried one windy Sunday afternoon of sunshine and drifting cumulus clouds. The summer breeze blew through the grass and bushes in the churchyard and got under the minister's cassock so that he had to stand and hold it down like some prudish woman, and the sound of the hymns came in waves so that at one time it was deafeningly close and at others almost completely inaudible in the blue depths behind the churchyard wall. Finally, Uncle Hans' girls' choir sang, *"My life is a wave"*.

Many tears were shed, and you yourself had to stand and grind your teeth to keep your emotions in check. But your sorrow was not so much due to Platen as to something quite different. For that very same day, you had been told that Merrit was soon to leave the country. Her father, who had been captain on the *Christina* for some time, was now to be captain of another much bigger ship sailing to the West Indies, and his wife and daughter were now to live in Copenhagen.

But you hadn't really had time to grasp the fact that Merrit was to go away and that your ways would part, perhaps for ever. After the funeral, you went up through the fields to the Willow Grove, and here you lay down in the grass and stared up into the moving skies while abandoning yourself to – well, to what?

***

To a certain pleasure containing an element of pain – that is probably the best way to describe it on looking back with the wisdom of old age – demonstrating the truth of the saying that the only really happy love is unhappy love.

Of course, you didn't think like that in those days. Your thoughts were warm dreams of desire and enamoured visions: see, there she comes, all in her summer dress with the wind in her hair (a reasonable description, though not quite right, for *myth* has already started to come into play with her).

"Merrit. Are *you* here?"

"Yes, 'cos I knew *you* were here."

And she sits down with you in the grass, smiling, but with red rings round her eyes, for she has been weeping. You take her hands.

"Merrit. I knew you'd come."

(Alas, this was all lies, sweet lies that are like stolen fruit that rots even before you have eaten it.)

"Amaldus. Won't you kiss me? Yes, like that." Whoo-oo-oo... now you are out floating with your *earth girl*.

(This was not a total fabrication, of course.)

And so we float out in the late summer's day, low over the soughing fields with all their nodding flowers, right out across the whispering heather on the dark heath... towards the west, towards the west where the sea extends quietly foaming and endless. And now the entire web of inventions is suddenly the truth, the truth because it has been endowed with the transcendental dimension of poetry!

Then the sea roars almightily below us, vast, stretching for mile after mile as I look into her green stare eyes and *love* her. And this continues into the ferocious, desolate evening space over the sea, and perhaps into eternity, indeed perhaps into death, for perhaps it will be best that we never, never return, but... but...

"*Amaldus*! Are *you* here?"

You look up and encounter Aunt Nanna's smiling eyes. Keil the photographer is standing behind her. They are both still dressed for the funeral, but Aunt Nanna's face is radiant. Keil has a camera in a strap over his shoulder.

You stay there lying in the grass completely flustered, wanting most of all to jump up and run off.

"No, stay where you are, Amaldus – we're only out to take a few snaps in the good weather, and you look so funny lying there all on your own and thinking."

There is the sound of a click, and there you are, preserved to all time with all your agony.

And so your yearnings and dreams are gone; they are as though torn to shreds by the wind and already far away in the blue sky.

***

But they come back; indeed, they will pursue you for years – like some unforgettable melody that is fixed in your ear and which you occasionally become aware of and lose yourself in – and at that moment nothing else exists except just this melody, for everything else (including what is known as unassailable reality) fades away and is lost...

Poetry always has the last word.

Embarkation in Cloudy Weather

At this point a brief account of the bitter leave-taking with Merrit as it played out on the grey stage of reality.

There is also a good deal of wind, but the sun refuses to shine, for it's an ordinary miserable showery day with banks of low cloud in the mountains and with the angry cries of gulls and the smell of sacking and canvas from the grey bales of fish being taken on board the *Christina* in salt-encrusted lighters.

And then there is the wretched green ferry. And the Ferryman sitting there, waiting at his oars, hunched up and miserable and without his horn.

And there, finally, come Merrit and her mother, both in hooded grey-green cloaks. Trunks and luggage are brought out to the boat, and then there is the leave-taking with friends and acquaintances. Merrit looks strangely hectic and bedraggled in a cloak that is far too big for her and flaps around her slender figure, and she is so busy that she has no time either to laugh or to cry – well, for a moment an expression of despair crosses her face when she embraces and kisses Grandmother. Then it is Jutta's turn, standing weeping for all to see: she is also given a kiss and a sisterly pat on the back. Then it is Mother and Aunt

Nanna and Little Brother... and then, finally, it is your turn: a quick little smile and "all the best, Amaldus". And then it is all over; it was nothing, nothing at all. And yet... for wasn't there something after all? A secret glint in the corner of her eye, almost imperceptible, and yet as precious as a diamond?

No, there was nothing.

And then the boat casts off and slowly disappears into the mist to the accompaniment of waving hands and handkerchiefs.

***

That little grey, misty figure among all the other shadowy figures in the boat as it glided away – was it Merrit, the wonderful girl, the girl who could catch the sun and hold a rainbow in her hand, the girl who danced with outstretched arms across the Life Bridge, the girl who gave you the first kiss in your life?

No, it wasn't her.

The real Merrit never went away; she remained for ever up in the green grasslands of summer; she is still there today and plays the melodic minor scale in the dusk beneath the lighted candles on the piano.

She is the Earth Girl, who takes you out on breathtaking trips, floating in the air to the End of the World.

She has become what everything finally becomes: Myth and Legend, Longing and Pain and – deepest down – profound, hidden, imperishable happiness.

The Steam Engine

The factory is going to be taken into use again and set going. There is a swarm of craftsmen and ordinary workmen out there; the rusty old machinery is being dismantled and new put in its place. Consideration is being given to whether the old steam-driven machinery should be taken out to sea and sunk or taken out of the country and sold as scrap iron, but for the moment it is being put on a kind of huge sledge drawn by black horses and taken down to the shore near the Ring so as to get it out of the way.

Here, it is stood up on end and looks very strange and alien in the middle of the everyday surroundings of the grey, lichen-covered rocks. There is a "manhole" down at the bottom in the big steam boiler, so that you can get into it. It isn't quite dark in there, as a cold, iron light seeps in from above, creating a kind of nightmare half-light, threatening yet strangely compelling.

So the big drum is here and is no longer a boiler but something else, something without name or significance – like something in a dream. Something that might remind you of the Tower at the End of the World, which of course is far bigger and more impressive. Or *was,* for it is not there any more.

No, the Tower at the End of the World is irrevocably a thing of the past – indeed, it has never even really existed! A strange, shattering, vertiginous idea both filled with a sense of release and yet full of melancholy. And so there you stand now, abandoned and numbed, in the dark interior of the old, discarded boiler... and outside the mists swirl above the rushing abyss where the spirit of God still hovers over the waters (for after all, no one can stop Him from doing this). It is sinister and lonely out here, indeed you could scream with revulsion, but yet you wait a little longer before escaping into the day and reality... you wait until you simply can't stand it any longer; you double up and stand there suffering until you almost die from fright. Then, with a howl of liberation, you climb out of the manhole and stand there in the light of day, thrilled with relief and delight, like a soul that has escaped from the powers of darkness and battled its way up from the tomb...

Just fancy that you are standing out there in the sunlight beneath a blue sky listening to the gulls screeching and seeing their wings flash in the air and casting fleeting shadows on the rocky surface. And on the drying grounds over on the other side of the Ring, the fisherfolk are busy lifting the heavy canvases and bast mats from the stacks, for now it is lovely dry weather so they must hurry to get the fish spread out in the sunshine. And Anton, the watchman stands with his telescope, looking out across the bay, where a heavily laden fishing sloop is on its way in.

But that game of terror in the tower is one you'll have to play once more before you go back to town. Once more, you have to squeeze into the iron night in there and suffer until you can't stand it any longer, and then laughing and gasping with delight, you dash back out into the sunshine and freedom.

***

When you think about it, it's probably a silly game and perhaps you are what you least of all want to be: *a feckless idiot*.

It's quite a different matter with Little Brother; no one would think of calling him *feckless* – he's a "bright lad"; he already knows his tables up to the ten times off by heart, and Father's starting to teach him up to twenty as well. As for you, you still find it difficult to remember them up to ten times – not to mention the *Reigns of the Kings and Queens*. And you can sense that your Father is afraid you might become a feckless idiot and good-for-nothing like Uncle Hans. For when he takes the time to sit down once more to tell you what the world is made of, you just sit there staring at his pipe and his big nose, and that feckless head of yours fails to make any sense of it at all.

For if the world is round and there are people living all the way round it, why do you never hear of anyone falling off?

"Because 'up and down' is something that only applies here and now. Out in Space there's no 'up and down', only out from and in towards."

And then we come to all these questions about the Moon and the Sun, the Tide and Currents. And Newton's apple.

Why an apple and not a pear? And why was it an apple and not a pear that Eve plucked from the Tree of Knowledge and gave Adam to eat?

Mother nods over her ironing and says she knows what you are getting at.

And then your thoughts wander from Newton's perfect apple to the egg that Columbus made to stand up by knocking the pointed end down on the table top. Surely that was a bit of a cheat?

Yes, Mother agrees. Like the story of Alexander the Great's knot.

"What knot was that?"

Then Mother tells the story of the Gordian knot that Alexander undid by slicing it with his sword. That was cheating as well.

And all that about the Earth rolling and sailing freely in the air – that's not far from cheating, either. 'Cos where is God's Heaven then, and where is God Himself?

Here, it is Father who can't really follow, but is content to sit with a frown on his face and at a loss for an answer.

Then he gets up with a brief laugh and stands with his hands in his trouser pockets, looking out of the window.

***

But the fact is that there are both bright sparks and feckless idiots. Bright sparks use their heads and decide what is to happen and how to deal with everything. They have a lot to take care of and worry about.

Feckless idiots, on the other hand – they don't bother about anything even though they get in the way both of themselves and of others and mess things up for themselves. They sing and hum and play the horn or sit rubbing their violins or feeding their ducks and sticking coloured paper on blown duck eggs.

Or they lie around dreaming and crying out in their sleep and then coming and telling hair-raising stories about what they have experienced in their dreams and wondering what this, that and the other can mean and "foreshadow".

Selimsen, the artist, writes his dreams down in a "night book" and keeps a count of which dreams come true and which don't.

That's ridiculous and disgraceful. Father and Michelsen the bookkeeper are agreed on that. And so, too, are the Numerator and the Denominator, as they call the twin brothers who come and play cards with Father and Michelsen. They are both navigation instructors and among the brightest sparks in town; they sit there with shiny foreheads and raised eyebrows and smile in their beards at all the wickedness of the world.

But they don't believe in God.

"And what will happen to the Numerator and Denominator on Judgement Day?"

Mother sighs and looks into space.

"Don't ask me, my dear, for I simply don't know. I only know that to God the Numerator and the Denominator are no more than two grains of sand on the seashore."

Exile

Father has an awful lot to see to at this time. It happens ever more frequently that he "flies off the handle", so that even Mother is frightened of him.

Now that the Factory is to be taken into use again there can no longer be a question of having concerts and balls out there.

The Feckless Idiots' Plot – such is the name that Father also gives to Uncle Hans and his friends. It's an unpleasant expression, this word "feckless", dead and clammy and tacky like putty. Keil is especially feckless – "and I'll make sure I put an end to his carrying on with our dear Nanna."

"Yes, but what about her, then?"

Father doesn't answer immediately, but he sits there thinking.

Mother (with a sigh): "It's a pity for Nanna. She's so much in love with Keil."

Father: "Being in love never lasts long. It's like a soap bubble. It's nothing to stake your future on. Why not Debes the Lighthouse Keeper? – She'd have been all right with him. Wouldn't that be a good thing? Debes is a widower and still in the prime of life."

Mother smiles quietly and shakes her head.

Silence.

Father (in a quiet voice and with his knuckles on the table): "I won't have that windbag Keil running around here. She *must* be able to understand that Keil's a man with no backbone. She's a sensible girl. And surely she must have learnt something from that ridiculous affair with Harry. I'll have a serious talk to her."

Then Father had a serious talk to Aunt Nanna on her own,

while Mother sat wringing her hands out in the kitchen.

Father (after the conversation): "Well, as I expected; your sister's a sensible woman, so it's possible to talk to her. She took it nicely."

But the following day Aunt Nanna had again made herself invisible and shut herself up in her room and refused to react to Mother's calling and knocking.

***

Selimsen the artist is a windbag and feckless idiot, too, and to a portrait he has painted of Uncle Hans sitting deep in thought on a boulder on the beach Father has given the title of "Toper by the Sea".

Mother (flushed): "But it's a good picture, Johan. It's a work of art."

"It might be a work of art. But Selimsen's still a filthy beast."

Father lights his pipe. His hands are trembling.

"Poor Platen, he was the most decent one of the whole crowd after all. At least he didn't go carrying on with women and getting them into trouble."

Mother (pleading): "But *Hans* isn't like that."

Father stares darkly in the air. Then he takes Mother's hand and whispers something in her ear, and she sits for a moment shaking her head, her mouth open and her eyes closed.

***

In spite of everything, Mother wanted to buy Selimsen's picture of Uncle Hans by the sea, and Father agreed to it. But the day Selimsen came with the painting, something *happened* in the office where the two men were alone. And when Father came in to dinner his face was very red and his look was very dark, and he was very silent.

The following day Selimsen and Keil left for Copenhagen on the *Christina*. They had been provided with money and a free passage, and their debts to the Rømer Concern had been written off.

Father (with a harsh little laugh): "Well, that was *exile*, Else. And so that's over and done with. But then there's *Hans* – our poor banshee."

The Banshee

Well then there was Uncle Hans, whom Father wanted to "drag up from the morass" and to "make a proper man of him".

"What's a banshee?"

Mother sits there staring ahead, and it's as though she can't pull herself together to tell you what a banshee is.

"It's something to do with a ship."

"What on a ship? Something about the rigging?"

"No."

"Something about the galley?"

"No."

"What then?"

Mother shakes her head.

"No, it's nothing like that. It's a kind of ship's ghost, or whatever..."

Banshee. A new word, both to laugh at and be frightened of. You'd like to go on to ask why Uncle Hans is a banshee, but you don't because you can sense it's something it hurts your Mother to discuss.

Nor is it just that Uncle Hans is going around as a banshee

and a feckless idiot with no "backbone". He must have done something absolutely awful. But what?

Hannibal knows, but he won't really say what.

"Cos I never gossip, you know."

But neither does he keep quiet, so he produces a few enigmatic phrases and leaves you to work out for yourself what he means.

It's something about Dolly Rose. And then it might be that Fina the Hut has been up to tricks with her magic spells, who knows?

***

Mother (one evening when you had worn yourself out over some sums that you were doing for homework and were leaning forward, tired out and with your forehead down on the table top):

"All this harshness is useless, Johan. You'll only make him hate you more and more."

You become wide awake on hearing this word *hate*. You think at first that it's about *you*, but you soon understand that she's referring to Uncle Hans; you remain motionless, listening.

Father: "You just keep out of it, Else."

Silence. Father walks up and down the floor.

Mother: "You can see where it's getting him, Johan."

Father (stops): "What do you mean?"

Mother silent.

Father: "What do you really mean by that?"

Mother (in a broken voice): "I mean — *Amaldus!* You'd better go to bed; you're just sitting there going to sleep."

So you went to bed, with a sense of unease and filled with foreboding.

***

Mother (in a letter to her sister Helene in Copenhagen):

"...This question of Hans is getting us all upset, and often making me quite unhappy, for you know how fond I am of him. Since Selimsen and Keil left he has gone around all on his own in some curious way and not had anyone to talk to except Mother. But of course he doesn't confide in her, and she doesn't encourage him to, nor has she really ever done, and so they probably only talk about music and 'the old days'. And as for his sisters, I think he's a bit embarrassed towards them because of that unfortunate affair with Rosa (Dolly Rose), Fina the Hut's daughter. I think you'll remember her as a little girl – she used to stand at Fina's garden gate, always beautifully dressed in red and white and with a finger in her mouth. She's now said to be five months gone, and Johan insists vehemently that Hans must take the consequences of his actions and marry the girl, but Hans won't.

He's hardly on speaking terms with Johan any longer. All conversations simply turn into monologues on the part of Johan, and it is pitiful to see how embarrassed Hans is by all the scornful and bitter things he has to hear, however much truth there might be in them. I understand he hardly ever comes to the office any more but hangs around entirely on his own or goes off in his sailing boat – and I'm concerned about that, because he has never been careful enough with that boat, and now he is worse than ever.

And in brief... as for his appearance, he is hardly re-cognisable, and has left his beard untrimmed. You can imagine how uncomfortable I feel when I'm together with him, for I would so much like to be able to help him. But he doesn't show any confidence in me either, and if I touch on this question of Rosa, he shuts up completely and refuses to say anything.

Then he tends to disappear and stay out all night – and where does he get to? Perhaps (it is to be hoped) he's together with Rosa, but perhaps not, for one morning our warehouse keeper found him lying on the floor in what is known as 'Rydberg's Bedroom' up in the loft in the green store; he was dead drunk and lay there frozen stiff, for it was during some cold weather. Father was like that occasionally, if you remember. Oh dear, I fear the worst..."

Catastrophe

October, equinox, south-westerly gale, dreadful weather.

The town lies there blinded and deafened in a fog of foam; jetties and fish-drying grounds are under water, and in many places the whitish green, foaming waters go right up into the streets and turn them into raging torrents. And even at midday it's so dark that you can only vaguely make out the outlines of the dismantled fishing boats moored out in the roads, tugging at their anchor chains. If their mooring lines don't hold they will be hopelessly lost in this onshore gale.

The 'bedroom' on the top floor in the end of the Green Storehouse is full of men dressed in greatcoats and fur caps standing at the window because that is the place with the best view, and Father is there with his long telescope. Everyone is shouting because of the din from the wind and the sea. The air rings with the names of all the ships threatened with destruction – *Only Sister, Sumburgh Head, Realist, Goodwoman* (all of them British ships bought in Scotland).

Inside, on the great sail loft there is such a howling and whistling of wind and clattering of shutters that Little Brother and I have to make signs to each other instead of shouting while, with the help of a rope hanging there, we try to get on to one of the crossbeams supporting the roof. All the woodwork in this great building is complaining and creaking and cracking and a mainsail lying stretched out on the floor is now and again overcome by dreadful convulsions.

I finally manage to get onto the beam. Up here under the roof I can lie on my stomach like some sort of god and look down on the vast landscape of the floor, where Little Brother is dancing up and down in fury at not being able to climb up here, the place he knows as the supreme dwelling place of earthly bliss and happiness.

But then something *happens*: men come rushing out of the bedroom door and disappear with a great rumbling down the stairs... and then you have to go down to see what is going on out in the world. And something dreadful is going on, for the sloop the *Goodwoman* has broken its moorings and is in danger of being driven ashore!

It was dreadful to see the well kept, newly painted ship running in on the breakers and finally coming to rest on its side, overcome, pressed violently against the rocks and with its masts sticking obliquely up into the air. And almost worse was the sight of Father's distorted face – he stood there with open mouth and showed all his big teeth in a massive smile, but it was a smile of fury and pain, and his eyes showed he was not far from tears.

From out in the surf there came some penetrating sounds sharp like shots; this was the ship's bowsprit being broken and shattered. But now it was already so dark that it was almost impossible to distinguish the poor vessel, which was now no longer a ship, but a wreck.

Not until morning was about to arrive did the gale abate.

In the growing light it was possible to see the pitiful stripped remains of *Goodwoman's* tortured hull, without masts and bowsprit and with a bared frame behind the splintered bows. Flotsam was being rocked everywhere on the great swell, and far up among the houses there lay bits of wreckage scattered among pieces of sea wrack and ramalia and dead fish.

***

There was not much to be saved from the wrecked ship, which had "met its fate" and now lay overturned and firmly fixed among seaweed-covered cliffs, with its keel sticking out of the water so that from the shore you could see the empty interior of the hull through gaps and cracks in the smashed deck.

The gale that night had wreaked havoc elsewhere as well; a lighter and two smaller boats had suffered the same fate as the sloop, and out on one of the drying grounds near the Ring one of the storehouses was without a roof. But all this was as nothing compared with the catastrophe that had occurred that same night off the steep mountainsides on the southern coast of the island, where a large foreign ship had gone aground and been wrecked – losing everyone on board.

It later turned out that it was a Dutch merchant vessel, the *Moorkerken* that had met this grim fate; but no one knew that at the time. In general, no one knew anything at all until wreckage from the lost ship and the first bodies of the drowned sailors began to wash ashore.

During the following days and weeks ever more broken bodies were washed ashore. They were sewn into sacking and taken to the porch of the church.

It was a time of dark days and pale faces and the slow ringing of church bells. The first of the drowned men to be buried were accompanied by a large gathering at the graveside; on the next occasion the assembly was smaller, and as for the last two burials, which took place in rain and sleet, the priest and the grave digger were the only ones present in the churchyard apart from the six pallbearers; but both Father and Michelsen and the two navigation instructors were among the pallbearers, as they wanted to do the "final honours" to the unknown drowned sailors.

Fate

Fate is and will always be the strangest of all words. Fate is the grimmest of all grim things. "Inscrutable are the paths of fate," "No one avoids his fate." Many people are, "pursued by an evil fate".

Gerlak's children are pursued by such an evil fate. It is with them as it was with the Window Man's children – they are carried away one by one when least expected, and then they *die*; there is no escaping it: they have "consumption", and that's their fate. This evil fate doesn't come at once, but it lies in wait. They jump around and dance, play and fight like other children and don't look at all different, but one day the cough catches them, and then "you know what to expect". The four eldest children have been taken by it, and now the next, a little ten-year-old girl is simply lying there awaiting *her* fate.

But the son, Karl-Erik, who is eleven, is still running around playing "Come home, dear birdie" together with other children, as though all was right with the world.

>Come home, dear birdie
>Come home, dear birdie

So sing the children, keeping good time and singing together, so loud that it echoes among the houses. But then, suddenly, it is as though it's no longer the happy playing children's voices you hear, but quite different voices – for now it's the dead siblings calling to Karl-Erik from their graves.

"You mustn't think so much about it, Amaldus. Those children are with God, and they are all right, far better off than they were down here on earth."

"Then why do they have to be down here on earth first and be ill and feel awful?"

"Well, I suppose there's a meaning to it, but we human beings don't understand that meaning."

But what if there isn't a meaning? And what if there isn't a God? A thought you daren't think, but which you think even so. And then for a moment it's as though you grew all stiff inside from sorrow and horror.

Gerlak the shoemaker lives in a tall, narrow house on The Steps, one of the steep alleyways leading down to the water. At the top of the gable looking out across the water is the little attic room where Karl Erik's sister Leonora lies ill, and as it grows dark you can see the lamp being lit behind the red curtain. The narrow gable stands out black and tower-like against the fading evening light in the west. Then the evening is filled with sorrow, sorrow and fate, sorrow and fate. Then you have to think about the Big Sluggish Beast that Merrit once told you about. Then it is that this strange beast with the sorrowful, begging eyes comes slowly along through the dusk.

Then it is good to see the Moon rising from the sea. Oh, just look how huge and red it glows behind the dark horizon in the east. For a moment it disappears in the clouds, but it peeps out again and reveals its delightful red face between the blankets of clouds, lying watching out there in its vast bed like someone lazing about and unwilling to get up. Yet before long it pulls itself together and sets out on its vast nightly expedition across the heavens, refreshed and in fine spirits. And so round, so round!

And the Earth is round like that as well. And the Sun. And all three of them, the Moon, the Earth and the Sun, all three of them sail along on circular paths around each other as though playing some magical and beautiful game out in the heavens.

Diamonds in the Dark

Low clouds, grey, sombre days.

Not all of them are just grey – some conceal remarkable colours. The drifting clouds have a touch of rust red, olive green, muddy brown or stone grey, and the light can have a hint of a cold blue like newly hardened steel. And the sun will occasionally reveal itself as it sets and emit a smouldering, subterranean light over the sea and the weather-beaten land.

***

It was about this time you were given your own room, a room in the loft with a sloping wall on one side. It had long served as a lumber room, but it had been cleared out now and painted and papered, and the floor had been covered with fresh linoleum. This linoleum had a pervasive smell that haunts your nose to this very day, a nauseating smell of affliction bordering on despair, and yet with an element of hidden delight: yes, thus and only thus, is the scent of your early youth!

By the window a worn and disfigured but solid old writing desk with an inkwell and a blotting pad and beneath the sloping wall an iron bedstead, and if it's cold in the winter there is a paraffin stove for you to light. In the dark, the patterned top of the little stove projects a delightful flower garden on to the sloping wall. In addition, there is an iron washstand with a wash basin and soap dish. There is a bookshelf on the upright wall and above this a tear-off calendar and a dirty, faded chart of the Norwegian Sea. There was originally a mirror, too, but you've put that away in a corner and turned it to the wall, for who in the long run can put up with the sight of his own dejected face with all those red spots on his forehead...

But the idea here is that you should be able to sit undisturbed and do your homework in peace and quiet and develop gently in the way of a hyacinth bulb in the half light beneath its pointed grey cover.

And you would perhaps have been able to find peace and quiet if external things had been all and you had not constantly been disturbed and alarmed by mystifying volcanic forces within you – disturbing dreams and delusive visions, disquieting, shapeless thoughts struggling furiously to escape from the imprisonment imposed on them by their immaturity.

The tear-off calendar on the wall, with its big, sensible numbers looks quite ordinary and harmless, but it could well be one secretly initiated in Fate's intentions. Fate holds all our days in its hand. The future is hidden in the block of slips yet to be torn off.

On the back of these slips there is an abundance of printed texts, a verse or a proverb, and if you have once decided that they are warnings and signs sent by Fate, they acquire a sort of magical power. One evening, with a beating heart you turn over the slips for your birthday, the 11th of June, to see what this oracle calendar might have to tell you about your own fate. It's a verse and you immediately see that it has something to do with "fear" and "death" and wonder at the last moment

152

whether it would perhaps be better to let the calendar keep its knowledge to itself. But then your eyes have been there after all and seen the message:

> I know now fear as ne'er before
> As though I stood at death's dark door
> And had to enter and fall down
> In darkness and in fear alone.
> Pushed forth I am with stormy haste
> O God, oh God, pray hold me fast.

Hans Christian Andersen

Mother (with a checked tea towel over her hair and her sleeves rolled up, busy mixing flour and egg yolks for a cake mixture): "Well, that's a lovely message, Amaldus. You should be pleased to read that on your birthday. And don't you go and worry about fate. Everything is in God's hand even so. He decides on everyone's fate."

"Even bad people's?"

Mother gives you a worried look.

"Amaldus, you are so good at reading, you ought to read your Bible a bit more. You can always find consolation in the Word of the Lord and learn from it."

Mother hesitates and as it were looks a little dubious.

"But you'd probably best not read everything, for there's a lot you don't understand yet. But read Genesis and Christ's parables."

"But what ought I not to read?"

"Well, the Book of Revelation for instance."

"Why not?"

Mother wrinkles her brow: "Because you simply wouldn't understand it. No one does."

"Does it say anything about Fate?"

"Yes, about the Fate of the whole world at the end..."

That sounded exciting, and you devoured the Book of Revelation and were whirled down into its yawning abysses with their mysterious sea monsters and angels blowing trumpets and its hosts and vials of wrath.

***

Then the curious thing happened that while you of course had to tremble and shudder, you fundamentally liked the Book of Revelation, this, the most violent and uninhibited of all fairy tales; indeed you gradually came to love it, the craziest of all biblical writings. The hair-raising visions not only filled you with fear, but also with a certain warm excitement like the one that comes over you during a great thunderstorm, or during the resounding silence that follows when the sea settles again and captures the tranquil, vast firmament in its mirror.

Even to this very day, I associate a festive sense of exuberance with the description of the Holy City, the dwelling of Eternity, where it is so bright that there is no need for either Sun or Moon. And the names of the costly stones with which the city walls are adorned, you can still remember in their right order far better than you can remember any times tables or reigns of the kings: sapphire, chalcedony, emerald, sardonyx, sard, chrysolite, beryl, topaz, chrysoprase, hyacinth, amethyst – all those lovely words, of which you then only knew emerald (Merrit's) and sapphire (Mrs Midjord's), and then hyacinth, although only in the sense of a flower...

"But what is sardonyx?"

"I've no idea. You'd better ask Grandmother."

"And chrysolite? And amethyst?"

"Well, amethyst is a violet-coloured diamond. Nanna, show him your amethyst."

Aunt Nanna fetches a brooch containing a bluish violet stone. It shines in the light from the dark, wintry afternoon sunlight and smiles like a gentle little eye.

"But unfortunately it's only an imitation. The amethyst's only glass."

Of course, Grandmother knows lots of jewels, although not all of them, but the ones she knows she looks up in a big book on the bookshelf. Then each of these costly stones is seen in its own colour and splendour, so you can clearly imagine the sacred walls' foundations in all their magical grandeur: the blue sapphires, green emeralds and bluish green beryl, the yellow topazes, the red sardonyxes and the olive green chrysolite, and the chalcedony, in which a whitish grey eye glows with a golden interior fire.

And still with your mind full of this glorious resplendence, you return to the melancholy and gloom of your miserable cave, in which confused thoughts and unread exercises await you, and where the little tear-off calendar hangs threateningly on the wall and boasts of its gift of prophecy...

The Wise Man in the Tower

Then there were the dreams. They flourished during this dark time as never before, the nocturnal ones as well as the daydreams, and some of them have still not quite faded – for instance the dream of the wise man in the tower!

This tower, the wise man's tower, doesn't stand at the end of the world, but in some distant and inaccessible place on the wide curvature of the earth. It is the dream of the Wishing Tower, a consoling waking dream to which you abandon yourself, yearning and with a mixture of sweetness and pain.

This Wishing Tower stands on the top of a mountain. There is always sunshine and a clear sky here, and the Wise Old Man sits up there in his round turret room with all his books and writings.

A spiral staircase leads from this chamber up to the cupola at the top of the tower, where the great star telescope stands.

The wise old man must have a name. *Tycho Brahe* is a good name.

Tycho Brahe was certainly not always a happy man while he lived on earth. From Miss Gudelund's history lessons at school we know that he was exiled and had to leave his two wonderful castles of Uranienborg and Stjerneborg and settle among foreign peoples in a distant land. But now he is happy in his sky tower...

We also know that Tycho Brahe had a nose made of silver.

When night falls on the world and the sky is filled with starry constellations, the wise old man stands at the open peephole in his sky tower and turns his telescope while enjoying breathing the night air through his silver nose, which sparkles in the light from all the distant twinkling galaxies.

He reminds one of the Old Poet; indeed, the two are fundamentally the same person; they have the same kind of silvery beard and black bushy eyebrows that go up into their foreheads when they abandon themselves to deep thought. And they are both finished with the world and its troubles and torments and smile at the foolish acts of the feckless and at the arrogant self-assuredness of the bright.

The old thinker and astronomer stands in his lonely tower and listens to the harmony of the spheres (there is something called that, something related to the melodic minor scale). The wise old man is so wise that he simply knows everything, rather like God, but in a different way, for he isn't just a distant, inscrutable spirit, but also a human being like the rest of us; he can laugh and hum, drink tea and perhaps drink beer as well, and he can have an afternoon nap, something that he needs when he has been up for a long time during the night.

Aye, this Wise Man knows everything; he has no need to lie in bed and sigh, with his face buried in his pillow and feeling all confused.

You like this dream about Tycho Brahe so much that you have to tell Little Brother about it. But Little Brother, who is now ten years old and also goes to school, isn't the right person to tell your dreams to. He looks askance at you and asks questions that put you off.

"How high is the mountain the tower is on?"

"It's very high."

"Yes, but how many *feet* high?"

"Eighty thousand or perhaps rather ninety, or perhaps a hundred thousand."

"Well then, how do you get up there?"

"You don't need to. You are simply *there*."

"Always?"

"Always."

"But how do you get food and all that sort of stuff up there?"

"It's brought up by balloon."

"Yes, but if the balloon bursts or catches fire, or if a gale blows it away?"

"There aren't any gales in that country."

"Well, but who *pays* for all that? It must cost a lot. Have you thought about that, Amaldus?"

And Little Brother shakes his head in despair and can't be bothered asking any more.

The Dream of the Magnetic North Pole

That was the dream of the wise man at the top of the mountain. It was a good dream; it covered a lot; and it still keeps coming back a generation later like some beloved old melody (the Sicilienne from Bach's flute concerto, which the Ferryman's son Hans used to play at that very time together with Grandmother!)

And then there is the dream of the Magnetic North Pole.

It's a nightmare, but not one of the worst kind, for it still has a happy ending.

You've heard your father and Michelsen talk about the magnetic north pole, that strange place up in the Arctic Ocean that all compass needles point to. But in this dream, the Magnetic North Pole is a huge crater in the ice, so deep that it stretches almost down to the fire at the centre of the earth, and this crater draws you irresistibly, more and more powerfully the closer you come to it. Ever more quickly you are swept through the stormy air and sleet across the whole expanse of the northern sea and onto the eternal ice and the Polar skies filled with the Northern Lights until you reach the fateful place where you are irresistibly drawn down into the depths.

Down here, right at the bottom, there is a raging warm current that sweeps you away on its waters, terrified and yet at the same time filled with an almost voluptuous excitement. The water isn't boiling, but it has a kind of reasonable temperature in which to bathe, and the strange demonic fish milling about everywhere down here and following the current are sorts of mermaids with fishes' tails and fishes' heads, but in the middle they have human shapes, with big wet laps. They wind in and out among each other in graceful curves while staring at you with ravenous lidless fish eyes, smiling at you with half-open fishes' mouths.

Now the river grows narrower and the current stronger until, with a deafening gurgling sound, it is drawn into a dark, narrow fissure in the cliff, so narrow that you know it's quite impossible for you to pass through it. Here you remain, firmly wedged; you can feel the rough, cutting edges of the cliff around your head and the sharp outlines of its teeth against your cheeks. But as you hang there, abandoned and terrified, your ears are filled with the sound of a huge cascade of loud, echoing laughter as though from thousands of girls' voices, and then the narrow passage opens out, the walls give way and bleeding and wearied, but with a sense of indescribable liberation you feel you are again gliding along in open water and being borne on gentle hands into the brightness of clear daylight...

The Dream of the Woman Suspended between Heaven and Earth

That was the dream of the Magnetic North Pole.

Then there is the dream of the woman hanging out there, the "Hanging Girl", also unforgettable despite the passage of many years.

The Hanging Girl is suspended on a sloping roof between heaven and earth, in an uncomfortable position, with her legs hanging out over the eaves. She does nothing to hold on, and is completely indifferent to the possibility that she could easily slip and slide down into the depths. Her head rests on her right shoulder, which is drawn up, and her hip rests on her limp right hand. Her left arm and hand are hesitatingly turned up, with half-open fingers hanging down. The semi-spheres of her breasts are pouring out over a thin piece of cloth that serves as a wet cover over her midriff. Otherwise, she is entirely naked.

The Hanging Girl's face hangs as well; her eyelids are half closed; her lower lip hangs down from her half-open mouth; she has a bow hanging down from her hair, limp and wet.

(Such is the picture of the Hanging Girl as it was seen on an old page that had been torn out of a book and which you found in one of the two drawers in the desk, and, as you have subsequently been able to ascertain, it is a reproduction of Michelangelo's famous "Morning" on the tomb of Lorenzo de' Medici.)

Your first dream about this woman was terrifying and you will never forget it: you are flying, as so often happens in your dreams; you are floating among some high roof ridges, and there, on a roof slope with beautifully carved barge boards is the Hanging Girl with her lethargic, self-abandoning face and limp arms and huge inert thighs. She moves reluctantly, as if warding you off and telling you to leave her alone, but as though guided by invisible but determined arms, you are led into her embrace, and then something terrible happens: all the hanging parts of her start to shake; she starts slipping and slides slowly out over the eaves, down into the bottomless depths, and you yourself slip with her into the boundless abyss and are lost in a kind of evil and abhorrent state of rapture...

After this dreadful enervating dream you are long oppressed by secret shame, and at the same time you are possessed by the vision of the huge hanging girl; her picture must be taken out time after time and examined by voracious eyes, be re-experienced bit by bit: the disconsolate, weak face with the apathetic eyes and the open, sagging mouth, the unresisting lazy arms, the body's landscape with the two arched curves of the breasts, the navel's lonely grave in the desert, the desolate nothingness of the lap that hides something incomprehensible but desperately attractive, riches at once blissful and revolting...

The Dream of the House of Weeping

In contrast to the dreams on which I have dwelt here, there were the actual evil dreams, the cold ones that crept up on me with their stony gorgon eyes. One of these dreams has imprinted itself on my memory with special force. There are no longer any playful elements of any kind in this dream, and it is only about horror and pain.

It is a raw winter's afternoon with a darkening sky above muddy roads, and the air is full of gently falling snowflakes. *What had to happen* is past, and people are on their way home. You can only see them as wandering shadows in the hazy air, but you quite clearly feel their reality, the live breath that comes from their mouths and nostrils, the cold that sits on their skin and in their hair and in their nails, the warmth in their blood and entrails, the salty taste of tears in their gullets. And you know almost of all of them for they are people from your everyday life: the Ferryman and his sons, the Wise Virgins, Fina the Hut and her Dolly Rose, Hannibal and his mother Anna Diana, the artist Selimsen, Aunt Nanna and Keil the photographer... and they all have that same cold and tired expression and are looking ahead with that same gaunt stare without taking any notice of you as you make your way in the opposite direction.

Then the crowd thins out. Finally, you are alone, and now you start to hear the moans from the *House of Weeping*. It comes closer and closer, but the twilight is now so deep that you can only just make out the church-like outline of the black building from which the prolonged sounds of moaning and weeping emerge.

Then you stand there petrified, listening to the plaintive sounds that rise and fall and finally congeal into a kind of dark, complaining choral song: at first moving and full of gripping harmonies; but then the singing turns into a wild and meaningless high descant wailing that jars and hurts your ears and is more than you can stand.

Here, the dream suddenly ends, and you wake up, drenched in sweat and filled with an agonising confusion; the alarm clock is ringing and you jump out of bed and turn on the light. It is a dark December morning, but the sky is full of clear stars.

Then you are down on earth again, surrounded by everyday life and ordinary goings-on. Yet throughout that day and during the following days and nights you are concerned by this dream, which can't simply be swept away as mere rubbish and something of no significance, but it has come with its symbol to stay with you for life.

***

Symbol of what?

You have thought about that a lot since. Perhaps a symbol of meaningless Fate – sorry Fate. At all events, you experienced this shattering and never since forgotten nightmare at the very decisive time when Fate for the first time took hold of your awareness and raised the shiny, inescapable blade of its knife before your eyes without your any longer daring to believe that the hand gripping the handle was that of a good and just providence .

Lambert the Watchmaker

God no longer sits on His floor up in the mountains carving sacred words on His tablets of stone, and no longer does He float like a cloud over the waters in the great abyss beyond the end of the world. Where is He now?

Everywhere. In heaven and on earth, in you, in me, in our hearts and in our thoughts. He is a Spirit. The minister preaches this from his pulpit, and the teacher of religion from his desk.

"What is a Spirit?"

Mother lowers her sewing and sits for a moment staring ahead with clouded eyes.

"I really don't know, Amaldus. And I don't think it's any use bothering about *that*. I believe God is good and kind and will help and preserve us if only we sincerely ask for His help."

"But there are people who don't pray and don't believe – not only the Numerator and Denominator, but people like Lambertsen the watchmaker as well."

"Yes, but don't you bother your head about that, Amaldus. We mustn't interfere in things that only concern God. It will all work out in one way or another even with Lambertsen. You'll see."

But perhaps it won't all work out with Lambertsen. Perhaps he'll be damned. The Wise Virgins certainly think he will. They come to see us and are served with chocolate in the small gilt cups.

"Aye, poor Lambertsen. He'll lose his soul if he doesn't repent before the Great Day."

Miss Louise, the oldest of the sisters, has a bit of skin from her drinking chocolate on her chin. The other sister, Matilde, wipes her mouth carefully with the tip of her serviette.

"Yes, and isn't it terrible to think of? To be banished into darkness for ever. Ugh, ugh."

Mother (shaking her head as though pleading): "Yes, Yes, but even so, although it's hidden from us human beings, don't you think God must have some secret plan when He lets Lambertsen be a doubter?"

Miss Louise (emphatically): "God has given us all free will. It's Lambertsen's *will* that's the problem. He refuses to believe. He's heard the message and knows what it's all about. He's no heathen. He's responsible for his own misfortune."

So Miss Louise is right and Mother simply sits there looking strangely dejected.

Miss Louise has got a fresh bit of chocolate skin on her chin. She sits there, sighing and staring straight ahead.

"But dear Else, how... now, you mustn't be angry, for I'm only asking – but what about your own husband, the Captain?"

Mother (ill at ease): "What about him?"

"Well, he never goes to church, of course, and there are those who think he's a non-believer like Lambertsen."

Mother: "Amaldus, I think you'd better go up to your room and do your homework, dear."

**

So you go up to your attic and rather uneasily watch the rain-drops dripping from the cornice and running down the window. There they are, growing until they are so big they have to fall.

The drops are Fates. Up in the clouds sits God, letting drops drip and Fates happen.

You sit staring at the drops of Fate until it's all so distressing that you can't stand it any more. Then you go out into the rain, where drips are still falling from all the eaves.

164

Lambertsen the watchmaker is as usual sitting by the window in his workshop with a pocket watch in his hand and some sort of a tube fixed to one eye. The edge of his high, stiff collar cuts into his double chin. How on earth can he put up with that collar? But he can, at least, and he only ever wears that kind of collar. That must be his choice.

Lambertsen stares through his magnifying glass into the delicate workings of the watch, just as God examines the human heart. But Lambertsen doesn't believe in God. He *refuses*. He is an atheist, and that is his unhappy fate.

***

Father (at the dinner table, with a very scornful look in his eyes):

"Lambertsen, that harmless old man, in Hell? (Laughs grimly into his beard.) Aye, they're priceless, the silly old lot."

Everyday Reality

Up in the Willow Grove, some leafless bushes and trees are reflected in the little pool of rainwater that has accumulated on the level patch where grass and sorrel stand waving in the wind in summer.

It has just been raining, and drops are dripping from the black branches and making rings in the water. The rings quickly grow bigger and disappear. They come and go, and where they meet they hurry to merge into each other. You never tire of watching the lovely game played by the rain rings in the clear water, and for a brief moment you almost feel liberated from the infinite sadness with which you are burdened. But only for a moment, and then you are again in the grip of that boundless melancholy, standing there helpless on a bleak day among the weeping branches.

***

The desperation of these young years was profound indeed – nameless, for there were as yet no words to express it. But the sight of the raindrops' agile game on the surface of the water can still today, paradoxically, produce in you a painful memory of the burden and gravity of the immense and unrelenting affliction of those young days.

But then there was *everyday reality* – you could always find consolation in that, and you always came back to it, often running, frolicking, in a kind of irresistible enamoured longing.

Everyday reality is today, yesterday and always.

Everyday reality is the smoke that rises at noon from every chimney and drifts away on the wind.

Everyday reality is a grey cat running across a road.

Everyday reality is plates on the table and hands that have taken hold of knives and forks. Everyday reality is the smell of steaming washing and soap suds from a cellar entrance, and of pitch and tar from a boat that is being repaired, and of carbolineum from a new fence, and of peat smoke and fermenting seaweed and lighted pipes.

Everyday reality is the rubicund fisherman Sigvald standing outside his privy buttoning his trousers while glancing briefly at the drifting clouds over the sea. Everyday reality is the little grocer Hans Olsen standing by scales that are almost in balance and holding two potatoes in his fingers.

Everyday reality is the disabled but always cheerful Juliane the sexton's wife, who sits everlastingly on her window seat in the Coffee House with a crutch shiny with wear at either side, shaking her head with a smile at the funny old ways of the world.

Everyday reality is when people say, "Oh, how nice that it's a girl this time when they've only had boys otherwise." Or: "Good heavens, how Mrs Berg the headmaster's wife is putting on weight." Or: "No one in this town can make coffee like Pouline." Or: "Good heavens, is old Rosenmeyer dead? Aye, I suppose we must all come to that."

The sailmaker's needle, the watchmaker's magnifying glass, the shoemaker's pricker, the smith's hammer, the joiner's plane. A lullaby in the twilight from a window standing ajar. A hearty yawn, a roar of laughter. Tender words in the dusk from two figures sitting on the great pile of driftwood out near the Bight. All kinds of chequered eiderdown covers and slippers that are left unused at night and carefree snoring and savouring of sleep, while the rain pours down the windows...

That is what Everyday Reality is in all its insignificance and power. It makes no claim to provide a solution to any puzzle; it only has its own excellent rhythm to offer. It's a welcome brief rest during a long and difficult journey towards unknown and disturbing places.

It's nothing to boast about, for it's only ordinary, but everyone knows it and clings to it and loves it.

Today, the 11th of February 1974, I am Sitting by an Open Window in my Cabin, looking

out across the world, entranced by the unusual beauty of this afternoon.

The sun is low in the southern sky above a brownish golden

sea, and in the east the snow-scattered mountain tops can be seen rising towards a sky that is pearl-like in its radiance and against which they merge and almost disappear, as though they were freely floating in the air. There is a gentle, acidic scent of moss and moisture, and the midges are dancing. But the barometer is low and a westerly gale is said to be on its way across the sea.

Such a quiet, spring-like hour in the heart of winter is something you embrace as a costly gift, all the more precious as of course you know that it will only be transient and capricious. Transient and capricious like the gift of life itself, you think. Before long, this entire mirage will be gone like a soap bubble bursting.

P.S.

Gone indeed – for me, Amaldus the Ancient, whose balancing act on the Life Bridge will soon be at an end, but not for you, young reader, who with open arms and a beating heart still dance your hazardous but joyful dance on the narrow plank across the abyss.

Vesta

We are approaching the end of these sidelights on Amaldus's childhood and boyhood and we are out on the edge of the mosaic of selected fragments by means of which we have attempted to establish and throw light on this little biography. But the grim story has still to be told of the two fearful enchantresses who turned up in the arena one day and wrought momentous damage, though this was at the same time accompanied by new and valuable experiences.

William Heinesen

***

Hannibal has not been heard of for some time; he doesn't go to school any longer, but he has grown up and is sailing as a ship's boy on one of the small coastal boats. But today he's below and can go ashore. He has stood waiting for you at the school gate, and it can clearly be seen that he has something on his mind, something he is dying to tell you.

We go down to the Bight, where certain changes have been made; the "robbers' den" in the old warehouse cellar has been abandoned, but Hannibal has found a new and better place to go to in a nearby boathouse loft.

"Now just you see how fine I've made it, Amaldus. But first you must promise me to keep your mouth shut about everything you see. Do you promise?"

Hannibal has an exuberant expression in his eyes.

"'Cos you see, Amaldus, I've got a *girl* up there, 'cos I've got engaged. And you can bet your life she's a fine girl. She's called Vesta. She's up there waiting for me, and I'm going to show her to you now, but then you don't have to stay hanging around, but buzz off as soon as you've seen her. OK?"

The triangular little loft is full of biting cigarette smoke. Vesta is sitting on a kind of sofa that Hannibal has made of packing cases and a new carpet runner. She jumps up and looks furious when she discovers that Hannibal isn't alone.

"Why have you dragged *him* in here with you, Hannibal?"

"Take it easy. He's my best friend, as true as steel, and besides, he's my cousin."

So Vesta brightens up and is nice, and Hannibal sits down by her and tickles her under her arms until she squeals with doting laughter.

Vesta is older than Hannibal, almost sixteen. She's a tall

girl, very thin and with delicate little teeth that make you think of the skull, the one the Old Poet said was the head of a girl.

"Show him your eyes, Vesta."

Vesta opens her eyes wide so you can see one is blue and the other brown.

"Have you ever seen *that* before, Amaldus? No, 'cos no one but her has eyes like that. And look here."

Hannibal suddenly pulls at Vesta's sweater, making it roll up like a Venetian blind, but she quickly pulls it down again and knocks him with her knee so that he takes his fingers off her again. But they both laugh; they actually curl up with laughter.

"Well, he saw them all right, Vesta; didn't you, Amaldus?"

"See what?"

"Oh, come off it."

Vesta sits with her eyes closed and her mouth open and is a little tired of laughing.

"No, but off you go, Amaldus, 'cos you've been here long enough now; hasn't he Hannibal?"

"Yes, you'd better go now, Amaldus, 'cos Vesta's come over all..."

You don't hear what it is Vesta has come all over, for she has taken hold of Hannibal's head and is holding her hand pressed against his mouth.

Then you leave and stand for a moment dazzled by the sun and its vast reflection on the water, shaken and confused by what you have seen. For you did see them all right, even if it only lasted for such a brief moment that it was almost nothing. You saw them clearly for a second – two live globes with something red at the middle.

"Hello, Amaldus," – there comes the sound of a cheerful voice behind you – it's Harriet, the Numerator's sandy-haired daughter. She smiles at you showing a row of big teeth in her freckled face.

"Are you waiting for Hannibal?"

"No."

She points her thumb behind you at the little window in the boathouse loft: "Have you been up there? Then you know whether Vesta's there?"

Harriet's eyes are dark – greenish blue – like beryl. Confused, you stare at her breasts swelling up beneath the frizzy jersey. They are bigger than Vesta's.

"Eh, Amaldus? Why don't you answer me?"

"Yes."

"Yes, what do you mean?"

"She's up there."

Harriet shakes her head and gives you a gently surprised smile with her beryl eyes.

"Heavens above, you do look strange, what's the matter with you?"

And she hurries on.

The Path of Sin

Then some time elapses, perhaps a couple of weeks, perhaps a month.

It's the dark winter days around the solstice, and an agonising twilight dominates your room as well as your mind, a harrowing ambivalence: on the one hand a crushing spiritual fear resulting from an increasing lack of confidence in God's goodness and power, indeed at times even a straightforward doubt about His existence. On the other hand a ravenous attraction to the temptations of this world, the promising mira-bilia of grown-up life, the foaming, inflammatory mysteries of love life.

One day, you are then again exposed to one of these external events which, although everyday and ordinary enough, you remember as unique and lastingly epoch-making...

It's Saturday afternoon, the day before Christmas Eve, and Hannibal is going to his secret place in the boathouse loft.

"Come with me Amaldus, we've got something to show you."

"What?"

"You'll see."

"Yes, but then tell me what it is. Is it something to do with Vesta?"

"No, it's something else. Come on."

"No, I don't think I want to."

"Oh, you're just scared, that's what it is."

You won't have that, and so you join Hannibal, full of misgivings, but also with a feeling as though an uncontrollable sparkler was going off in your heart.

It's pitch dark up in the tiny loft, but the sound of giggling emerges from the gloom. It can't be coming from Vesta alone, so there must be another girl there as well, perhaps several.

You stand at the top step of the narrow stairs, hesitant and embarrassed. Then you feel a pair of hands grasp yours and pull at you – you can feel they are not Hannibal's rough paws but sticky, soft girl's hands tugging at you and trying to get you up through the trapdoor. For a moment you think of running away, but you can nevertheless not bring yourself to liberate yourself from these, eager, thin hands and so you chance it with a beating heart and tightened throat.

Then Hannibal lights a little Christmas candle; faces appear out of the gloom; big shadowy wings unfold on the knot-filled beams below the sloping wall, and subdued but intimate

172

laughter is directed at you from three triumphant mouths – Hannibal's, Vesta's and Harriet's, for it is *her* hands that have pulled you up through the trapdoor. She is smiling at you with warm beryl eyes.

Hannibal is sitting on the "sofa" with his arm round Vesta's waist.

"And now! We'll put the candle out again, 'cos we don't want all that light."

He blows the light out.

"Comfort him a bit, Harriet, 'cos he's awfully afraid of the dark."

"No, I'm sure he's not. You aren't, are you? Amaldus?"

You can feel Harriet's breath against your ear. Her arms around your neck. Her whispering mouth against your cheek. The enticing scent of her hair. The slight pressure of her breasts against your jersey. Her wheedling voice, for she is talking to you as though you were a kitten or a little lamb.

"Amaldus. It's only me, you know. Oh, what's wrong, Amaldus? Are you going?"

You have gently moved her arms from your neck and have drawn back, for you *are* really afraid, indeed you aren't far from tears because of an undignified feeling of perturbation and nervousness.

Giggling from the sofa. Vesta: "Is he going?"

Hannibal: "Yes, 'cos I told you he was frightened. He's never kissed a girl before."

No – *frightened?* You weren't having any of that. And suddenly, you really *aren't* frightened. You grasp Harriet's hands, hold her slender figure tight and kiss her – on her neck, her eyelids, her mouth, all over her face until she is almost out of breath.

"Amaldus! Oh no! Listen – you mustn't. Not like that."

173

Hannibal's voice from the darkness: "Well that got him going. Just you carry on, Amaldus."

Trembling, you gasp for breath; you have pushed your hand up under her jersey and are squeezing one of her breasts while still kissing her mouth, tempestuously, ceaselessly.

"Oh no," comes the sound of her voice, this time no longer subdued, but loud, almost scolding in tone: "Not like that. No more. You're strangling me."

Then you suddenly let go and push her away. You are trembling all over; there are tears in your eyes, and you have to fight to subdue an idiotic sob.

Harriet (out of breath and complaining): "Light the candle, Hannibal."

"What the hell are you two up to?"

Hannibal jumps down from the sofa, but before he manages to light a match you are out through the trapdoor and hurrying down the ladder, for you don't want them to see that you are more or less crying. It has been like the dream of the Hanging Girl – you're just about dying from shame and fright and a sense of something ignominious and unclean.

It's pouring with rain; you hurry home through the empty alleyways near the harbour, overcome with sorrow and regret, but still possessed by memories of the captivating scent of her hair and skin and breath and the soft curves of her breasts in the palm of your hand. A sad melody runs through your head, a couple of lines from an old hymn you learned when a small child:

> O gentle God, to Thee we pray,
> O keep us from the path of sin today.

"Amaldus. Have you gone to bed? You're not poorly, are you?"

It is your mother. She comes and sits down on the edge of

the bed and places a flat hand on your forehead. You shrink beneath her caresses, and for the first time in your life you wish she would go to hell.

"Does it hurt anywhere?"

"No."

"Don't you want your supper?"

"No, thank you."

"Hm."

This closed sound, *hm* – you sense what it means. It means that in some mysterious way she knows everything; she has guessed and worked it all out. She gets up with a sigh, but without asking any more questions.

"Have a good night's sleep, Amaldus. You'll get over it."

You didn't get over it; it got worse.

You have to make an effort and play a part to ensure that no one sees anything unusual about you; but you daren't look Mother in the eye. Perhaps Harriet has told everybody; perhaps the shameful affair is already known all over town.

On Christmas Eve, a dark, foggy day, you go to find Hannibal down in the harbour; he has just rowed his skipper and first mate ashore from the moored motorboat and is on his way home with a canvas bag over his shoulder.

"I'm glad I met you, Amaldus, 'cos I've got something very important to say to you."

"Oh, what about?"

"About Harriet. Come over here, we'll sit on this log."

Hannibal throws the bag down. He has adopted the air of a chieftain today and looks serious and authoritative and it makes you shudder.

"Tell me first what you did to her, Amaldus."

"What do you mean, did?"

"I mean, you got hold of her somewhere and *tore* her and

made her bleed."

"I did? No."

"Well, you *bit* her or something."

"No, I didn't bite her. Why are you asking? Was she bleeding?"

"No, I don't say she was bleeding. But you did something or other, for she was down on the floor crying after you went. Oh well, perhaps she was only crying because you buzzed off. What did you do? 'Cos she's absolutely crazy about you, quite daft. Understand? Well, you mustn't leave her in the lurch, but do the same as I've done with Vesta and get *engaged* to her. But then you'll have to be careful and not make a fool of yourself, 'cos she says you're the sort that can easily get a girl into trouble."

"What do you mean, *trouble*."

"Well, you fiddle about with them and then they're going to have a kid – like Dolly Rose with our uncle. For with all due respect to him, he's a clumsy twit when it comes to girls."

Hannibal gets up and swings the bag over his shoulder.

"You understand, Amaldus, that I'm only saying all this to you to *warn* you, 'cos you've still got a lot to learn, such a lot. And you're welcome to come up in my loft with Harriet, but then you must promise me to behave decently and not like a hungry wolf. Promise? Yes or no? Why don't you say anything?"

"Yes."

"Good. 'Cos I'll tell you something important: I'm responsible for both you and for her, and I won't run away from that. And then just you think on that, Harriet's a decent girl, and it's *brave* of her to risk coming up into our loft, 'cos her father the Numerator's a terribly strict man, and do you know: sometimes when he's angry, he beats both her and her brother with a swab. Well, shall we say we'll get together on the evening of the twenty-eighth at eight o'clock, eight sharp, up in our den? And I'll make sure Harriet is there as well so you can apologise and explain yourself to her."

Young Pain

On Christmas Eve you slipped out for a while and climbed up on The Window Man's turf roof, where you had a good view of the lighted windows in the Numerator's house in Step Street. You sat up there, hidden in the grass trying to catch a glimpse of Harriet through your father's telescope, but all you could see was confused shadows against the yellowing roller blinds with their prints of Rosenborg Castle and the Round Tower. So you sat there in the raw south wind that was blowing in from the sea and shivered, overwhelmed by the thought that you would soon be meeting again and perhaps become engaged like Hannibal and Vesta.

In the afternoon of the 27th, you had made up your mind not to keep the agreement with Hannibal. But when evening came, you couldn't resist tiptoeing out to the Bight and standing hidden in a corner to look up at the little window in the boathouse gable.

There was a gentle thaw that evening. The inspection ship the *Neptune* was out in the roads, reflecting its lights and lanterns in the dark waters. Now Harriet was surely up in the den waiting for you. Perhaps she was crying with longing, and that would really be a pity. You imagined how Vesta and Hannibal were laughing at her because she had been "stood up".

So the upshot of it all was that with a heart overflowing with the most delectable sense of pity and intoxicated with wild anticipation you slipped into the boatshed and, as though in delirium, you climbed up the narrow ladder leading to the loft...

Hannibal was there alone.

He was sitting on the edge of the sofa, leaning forward, with his legs wide apart and with a dead cigarette hanging from his lips. The candle, which was lit on the table, flickered in the draft from the open trapdoor so that his gigantic shadow moved on the sloping wall as though in exasperation.

"Shut the trapdoor, you idiot."

"Haven't they come yet?"

No reply.

"But it's well past eight o'clock."

Silence. Only the sound of waves lapping the shore.

"But I thought..."

"Yes, but you're a silly idiot."

Hannibal managed to light his cigarette; he drew his legs up and lay there puffing clouds of smoke in the air.

Then he started talking, slowly and in a broken voice, as though he didn't care whether he was understood or not.

"Well, Amaldus. As for Harriet, she just a quite ordinary bit of cheap fluff, and besides that she's a mere baby; she's only a schoolgirl, so you simply don't need to bother your head about her, and besides, you can be glad you didn't get engaged to her, 'cos that would just have meant a load of trouble. But it's different with Vesta, 'cos she's a grown up girl and we (and here Hannibal's voice broke a little) we've mixed our blood like you and I did that time. Well, I'm telling you everything as it is, and I am relying on you to be my true friend and not to go around gossiping."

Long silence. Waves lapping the shore. The distant sound of oars. Still further away the distant sound of music from the Temperance Association dance hall.

Hannibal gets up on his elbow and through the clouds of

smoke stares at the flickering flame of the Christmas candle.

"Do you know where they've gone? It's not difficult to guess. They've gone to the dance. *Do you get it?* And they're not coming here this evening at all. They're not going to come here any more."

"But how can you be so sure of that?"

Hannibal makes a sweeping gesture with his hand.

"Because Vesta's said so herself. Can you keep a secret, Amaldus?"

"Yes."

"Then I can tell you it's all off between her and me. She was here yesterday evening – no, she didn't come up. She just stood down there and shouted up through the trap door and said that it was all over between us for good now. And do you know why? Because she's gone crazy on one of the sailors from the *Neptune*. He's the cook's mate. I know him. He's a silly idiot and a dreadful show-off. And he's a shrimp as well. I could make mincemeat of him, and I might do that as well. Or blow the pair of them up."

Hannibal flicked the evil-smelling cigarette end away and stubbed it out under his shoe. Then he sat down again on the edge of the sofa and sat leaning forward, all morose with his face hidden in his hands. He was sniffing a little. But suddenly he got up as though he had made a sudden decision. He climbed up on the sofa and took hold of an oblong package that lay hidden in an old bag on the rafter beneath the sloping roof. It was the *maroon*.

"Have you still got that, Hannibal?"

"Of course."

"Is there real gunpowder in it?"

"Yes, of course, what the hell do you think otherwise? Do you think I've been lying?"

"Yes, but Hannibal..."

Hannibal gave a bitter laugh, but there was no sign of a smile.

"Never in my life did I think she'd have to suffer for it."

"What do you mean by suffer for it, Hannibal? Are you going to blow her up, or what?"

"Blow her up? This evening? Now you're talking like the silly idiot you are."

"Yes, but you said 'suffer for it'. That's what you said."

"Did I say that? Oh no, I could never make myself do that. I don't wish her any harm. I only wish her well."

Hannibal sits with the maroon on his knees, stroking the dreadful bomb as though it were a kitten.

"No, honestly, I don't wish her any harm, not the least little bit. I only wish her well."

"Well, what then?"

Hannibal climbs up again and carefully pushes the maroon back into place.

"I don't wish *him* any harm either. Him, the cook's mate. I just wish them both well."

Silence and curious strangled sniffing.

Then he gets up again and raises his threatening fists up in the air. He has once more assumed his old chieftain's look.

"You see, Amaldus, my only true friend. This man standing here has the power to crush and destroy and pulverise them both – not even only them, but the entire Temperance Association building, where they're dancing and carrying on without the least suspicion. But he's *not going to*, for he doesn't wish harm on anyone. Never forget that I said those words, Amaldus. One day when I'm dead and gone, perhaps when I'm lying at the bottom of the sea, you'll remember what I said this evening. Promise?"

"Yes, Hannibal, I promise."

"That's good, Amaldus. Let's go now. Come on."

"Come where?"

"Come on."

***

The sounds of cheerful dance music and the hum of many voices emerges from the illuminated open windows of the Temperance Association. In the shadow beneath the stairs there are two drunken men taking it in turns to drink from a bottle.

"Here, Amaldus."

Hannibal has clambered up some railings from which it is possible to get hold of the eaves of a small outbuilding and swing up onto the roof. There, you can lie and look straight into the thronging dance hall. We lie on our stomachs, hidden in the dry winter's grass, lying completely still and watching. The dancing couples can clearly be seen, one by one, as they pass the open windows. We know almost all of them, all except the foreign sailors. But there is no sign of Vesta and Harriet.

Hannibal, whispering: "It almost looks as though they're not here, doesn't it. So they're probably already carrying on somewhere. No. See. There they are."

"Where?"

"They're on the stairs, damn it. And now they're going downstairs."

Yes, you can make them out in the crowd of young dancers going in and out: Vesta and Harriet, each with her sailor. They stop for a moment at the bottom of the stairs. The sailors offer them cigarettes. Harriet's face in the sharp light of the match. Beryl eyes...!

Hannibal (with a stifled, powerless hiss in his voice):

"There, you can see what they're like, the harpies. Just look how keen Vesta is, the bitch."

Vesta and the cook's mate quickly disappear into the darkness, arm in arm.

But Harriet, she's not so keen; she struggles and refuses to go with her sailor, standing still and holding on to a fence.

Your heart is beating and thumping in your chest and trying to get up into your mouth. No, she simply *won't*. It's no use the sailor pulling at her.

And yet, then she changes her mind. The sailor holds tight on her arm and she goes with him, unresisting, shaking her head... like a reed bending before a gust of wind.

You wish with all your heart that they could come up against the Numerator. You wish he could give that sailor one in the eye and drag his daughter off home and give her a real going over with the swab.

"Come on, Amaldus. *After them.*"

We jump down off the roof and stealthily follow the two couples, who are on their way towards the harbour. And then they go on towards the Redoubt. The sailors have their arms around the girls' waists. Now Vesta and the cook's mate stop; he hugs her, indeed he kisses her, in the middle of the street, beneath a lamp, long and tenderly.

Hannibal suddenly stops and doesn't want to go any further.

"Come on, Amaldus. Let's go in here instead."

He disappears in the dark narrow space between two boathouses, standing there and gasping, no longer even trying to hide his tears.

"Oh, the bloody bitch. They're *my* shoes she's wearing, the little hussy. I gave her all my savings to buy them. Aye, the shoes and then a pair of stockings and a bra as well as the floor runner up there, you know. What the hell did she want with a bra? Just tell me. Her breasts aren't so damned big that they need anything to hold them. That's what I told her and that's what she got so mad about, and that's what started it all. It really didn't take more than that."

Hannibal bursts out in an unpleasant sobbing laugh.

"But just you wait, you lousy bitch. Just you wait and see what's going to happen. And *you'd* better go home, Amaldus. 'Cos I want to be alone now."

"Yes, but..."

"Just go. 'Cos you're all right. You weren't engaged. You hadn't risked anything. You hadn't spent anything. It was nothing at all in your case. No, just you buzz off, Amaldus. I won't say it again."

And so you go, and Hannibal stays behind alone in the dark alleyway. To your consternation, you hear him abandon himself to lonely tears.

The Explosion

How things progressed further with Hannibal on the unfortunate evening of the 27th is something you heard from his own lips the following evening to your great and genuine sorrow and anger.

Your poor friend had first remained for a long time in the dark alleyway, torn between despair and an insatiable thirst for vengeance, but then he had made a quick decision and had gone over to the Redoubt, where the faithless Vesta and her cook's mate were sitting on a bench in a close embrace.

"And you see, Amaldus, I could have crept up on them and crushed the wretch from behind. But that would have been cowardly – well, you know what I'm like – no one shall ever be able to say that I was a sneak that came from behind – and so I said, 'Ha'.

They had a shock, and the cook's mate got up and looked at me, foolish like. Then I said, 'You go off, Vesta, for this is something between him and me.' She wouldn't, and so I went for him and knocked him down, and that was perhaps the daftest thing I could have done, 'cos now listen here: *Vesta* went all mad and started pulling my hair and scratching my face, and of course I made no resistance, for I'll never lay hands on a woman, you know, however brazen and shameless she might be, so I simply turned my back on her and let her get on with it. But by that time the bloody cook's mate had got up on his feet and he came at me from behind and knocked me down, and then they both went for me, and that bitch Vesta got hold of a piece of wet turf and rubbed me all over the face with its muddy side so I was completely blinded, and then they both trampled on me as I was lying there. But the worst of all was what Vesta said at the end, for do you know what she said? She said, 'You just lie there, you mad wretch, for you're crazy like Howler Hans your father, and you'll probably end up in the *klink* like him'."

Hannibal was breathing deeply, and he shook his head in silent torment.

"Aye, those were her last words to me, my fiancée, the girl I've spent everything I had on, you know. But all I can say is *Thank God*. Thank God that I finally got to know her. And if she comes back, 'cos she probably will, 'cos that's what she's like and that's what *all* women are like – if she comes back after she's got fed up with *whoring* with that stupid cook's mate, well (Hannibal put his hand up to his heart) – the key's been turned in the lock here!"

He got up, quickly rolled up the rug and lifted the lid from one of the boxes it had been on.

"Look here."

He thrust his hand down into the box: "Fireworks. She and I bought them together when things were still fine between us. We were going to have a real show on New Year's Eve. Look, there are both rockets and Bengal Lights and Jumping Jacks, and that damned lot cost me over ten *kroner*. But she's got another thing coming about those rockets, 'cos now it's going to be you and me celebrating New Year. And do you know what: we're going to let the *maroon* off as well. See, I've got a new piece of touch paper, 'cos I don't think the old one was any good. That's going to be some bang. It'll give the whole town a shock."

"Yes, but where will you let that bomb off, Hannibal?"

"Your voice is trembling, and I can well understand that, 'cos it's going to be *terrible*. But you needn't be scared; I'm not going to harm anyone, least of all *her*. So we'll go up on the Ring with it all, and we'll let the fireworks off first and then the maroon at the end. OK, Amaldus? Aren't you looking forward to it? Why don't you say something? Aren't you *looking forward to it?*"

"Yes, of course I am."

***

The terrifying events to be recorded here finally took place on New Year's Eve 1914 (the same year, incidentally, as our irresponsible contemporary on a higher plane, Kaiser Wilhelm II, set his infamous Great War in train).

To begin with it all looked as though it was going to be great fun (in both cases). There was a light, frosty breeze blowing from the north, and from the hilltops near the town and from promontories and spits down by the dark waters the red New Year's bonfires were flaming, while rockets drew their fiery arcs in the starry evening sky. Hannibal and his old friends and co-conspirators had brought a big old tar barrel out onto the beach near the Round, where it stood lighting up and crackling in a mighty froth of sparks and sweet tar smoke, while jumping jacks and Chinese crackers were merrily going off on the rocky ground and rockets were shooting up into the sky and spreading clouds of fiery dust down over the bay. We had the maroon hidden in the old steam engine; it was to be kept until the solemn stroke of midnight, and then it was to explode inside the drum and blow the whole machine to smithereens.

It gave you a strange bloodthirsty feeling to be inside the doomed drum, where a sole Christmas candle burned and the dreadful grey roll with the white touch hanging out lay on a box waiting for the fateful hour. No one was to be allowed in here except, for a moment, Karl-Erik, because according to Hannibal: "We must let him experience as much as possible in his short lifetime."

Hannibal looked at his watch.

"There'll be no steam engine here in half an hour. Then there'll be nothing left except perhaps a few bits of splintered iron, perhaps not even that. And it will go off with such a huge bang that everyone in town will have a shock. And a lot of people will be so scared they'll pass out."

Karl-Erik crouches outside the manhole; he only ventures to put his head and hands inside.

"Who's going to light the fuse, Hannibal? Are you?"

"No, you're going to, of course, Karl-Erik. Are you my *hajduk* or are you not?"

Karl-Erik turns pale and pulls right back from the manhole, but Hannibal has grabbed his jersey and holds him.

"You silly twit! Of course *I'm* the one that's going to light the fuse. What were you thinking of me, you silly fool? Have you ever in your life seen me behave like a bloody cook's mate? Yes or no?"

"No," Karl-Erik assures him, though he still dodges away and disappears in the dark.

Then comes the midnight hour and the great turn of the year. It feels like something with vast wings unfurling out in the darkness high above the world. Hannibal has his chieftain's look about him as he issues loud orders to everyone to keep away from the steam engine and to stay in safety behind the warehouses at the end of the fish-drying ground.

"*You* can stay and look into the manhole, Amaldus, if you dare, 'cos it's jolly dangerous. Dare you?"

"Yes."

You kneel in front of the manhole, trembling with anticipation, and you see Hannibal strike a match and put it to the fuse.

Then off you go as fast as you can – with a strange smell of catastrophe and the end of the world in your nose.

"Here, Amaldus. Lie down flat."

We lie down on the bottom of a deep fissure in the rock.

"Keep your mouth open, otherwise you'll get your eardrums burst."

So you keep your mouth open and can quite clearly hear your heart croaking in your throat. Perhaps this is your last hour, the hour of doom, the hour when the world will come to an end... and, as though in a terrible nightmare, you see before you in your mind's eye the *Tower*, and the lone cloud out in the void above the abyss, God's vast face with the angry eyes...

But the great crash heralding the end of the world fails to materialise.

Hannibal: "Hell. The fuse must have gone out. Or what else can have gone wrong? Perhaps the gunpowder's too old?"

There are the sounds of various crackers and bangers from in town, but they are only the ordinary ridiculous toy bangers you can buy in the shops.

Hannibal's voice shows him to be on the verge of tears.

"I've never known anything like it."

"But it might still come. Perhaps it's just smouldering."

"We'd better go up and have a look."

"Wouldn't it be better to wait a bit?"

So we lie there and wait a little longer. Hannibal sighs heavily and in distress.

"We *saw* the fuse caught, didn't we? Didn't you see it catch and turn black? So it must be the gunpowder that's lost its strength after all."

"Is it very old?"

"Aye, you bet it's old. It's from my Father's time."

Hannibal leans back against the wall of the chasm and sits there with his arms hanging limply at his side and staring at the sky, where there are still a few rockets to be seen rising and exploding against the dark background. He is in pain, and he is suffering. He almost looks like an old man.

Then he suddenly gets up.

"Come on."

He has already swung himself out of the chasm and is on his way towards the steam engine. You daren't follow. In the pale light from the stars you can see his watchful shadow approach the red light issuing from the manhole. The round patch of light looks like a rising moon that has just detached itself from the horizon.

Now he is crouching in front of the manhole. Now he's creeping inside it. You tremble with excitement and horror, clutching the cold stone and quite unable to move. For suppose it happened *now*.

But still nothing happens.

So it *has* failed. And thank God for that.

"Amaldus."

Hannibal's voice sounds broken, like a complaint.

"Amaldus. Where have you got to? What the devil are you frightened of? It's all spoiled. Have you got any matches?"

"Yes, but what for?"

"For a cigarette. I've used all mine."

Hannibal is standing there leaning against the rusty sides of the steamroller, drenched in sweat, his face all black and with a strange dead look in his eyes and with a fresh cigarette hanging from his lower lip. The Christmas candle has just about burnt down. The maroon is lying on its box amidst a pile of dead matches and scraps of paper and twisted bits of rope. The cover has been broken open with a knife; some black grains have spilled out and are lying there looking for all the world like burnt coffee beans.

Hannibal lights his cigarette. He gives a deep sigh.

"So it went all wrong, Hannibal?"

Devastated, he nods through hungry clouds of cigarette smoke.

"Had the gunpowder got damp?"

"Not a bit. It was just too old. Damn it."

"Wouldn't it catch?"

"Yes, just a bit. But nothing really came of it. It was just a silly idea."

"Isn't that smoke coming from the package?"

"Smoke? Oh yes, there's a bit. But it isn't *that*."

"Don't touch it, Hannibal."

"Nothing's going to happen. You can see the packaging's

broken open. It's only a bit of paper that's smoking."

Hannibal draws his dagger from its sheath, goes over and stirs the gently smoking paper.

"No. It was just the paper smouldering a bit."

But this is when it *happens*.

Not the great explosion. Only a long, sniggering, spluttering sound and a shower of sparks that sting your face, and a vast cloud of suffocating smoke...

And then... at the very last moment... out of the manhole, gasping for breath and with vicious pains all over your face and hands.

And Hannibal's voice, choking with the smoke: "We could easily have got caught out there."

Then, profound silence and darkness. And voices in the dark. But finally only a desolate whispering noise that gradually dies out.

The Generous Dark

After that fateful and unforgettable New Year's night, a new and equally unforgettable time dawned – a time in darkness, or at least in deep twilight, for you lay in the hospital with ice on your eyes.

It was nevertheless a time that only awakens happy memories when you look back on it, indeed it often produces something like a deep sense of enjoyment, linked to the smell of iodine and carbolic and – especially – the scent of steaming camomile tea that you had to breathe in for some reason or other as you lay there.

Then there were the sounds. The sound of footsteps, the chinking of glass and metal and crockery, the assiduous, helpful bustle of the hospital, gentle authoritative voices of the nurses and of Doctor Metze. And Hannibal's for he is in the same ward with burns all over his head and his hands, but although it is very rusty, his voice has taken on a new and almost cheerful sound. And the sound of other voices, all those heard during visiting hours and which have also acquired a new quality, a sort of strange new polish that makes it seem as though this is really only the first time you've noticed them. In particular Mother's, which (as you can hear) has adopted what seems to be a far too comforting and encouraging tone (so perhaps you are going to be blind after all). But you nevertheless liked to hear this loving voice feigning that all was well rather than Father's wordless humming and hawing – the only way in which he expressed himself during this period.

Then there were the sounds from outside that you could hear in quiet moments between sleeping and waking: the lapping of the waves on the nearby shore, the sound of oars, the squeaking of ropes and tackle, the screeching of falling anchor chains, the hoarse but self-assured hooting from the funnels on the steamship Mjølnir, the striking of the hour from the church tower on the other side of the bay... all these sounds from the light world that was no longer to be seen, but which was soon to emerge from the darkness, for the encouraging news was that, "It is not your actual sight that has been damaged, so you will soon be able to see again; you just need to be patient."

And then there was that unforgettable feeling of gentle hands in the darkness, of the riches they radiate. Your mother's hands on yours – a gift more precious than sun and moon. But also Sister Mette's hands when with firm but gentle fingers she opens your eyelids to drip in eyedrops that sting but heal.

Then, one day you are taken home and once more you lie in your familiar gable room, but still in the dark or at least in semi-darkness, for the window is covered with a green curtain.

But outside it's spring and brightening days, and from the starlings' nest up in the gable there comes a constant sound of the indomitable squawking and chattering of the first brood of hungry starling chicks. And Aunt Nanna comes with a little bunch of crocuses that she holds up to your nose so you can sense the sweet smell of earth and rain and *outdoors* coming from the cool petals.

What more?

Greyish green twilight days and black nights.

Waiting.

Did you lie there bored and boundlessly impatient? Did you lie there frightened and a prey to despair and sad thoughts?

You probably did, but there is almost nothing left of this in your memories. For those who lie and wait for the return of light and life live cheek by jowl with happiness, and the abundance of their expectations scarcely leaves room for worry. All the cares and tribulations are pushed aside for the moment and are piling up to provide problems in the future – just not *now*, now in the sheltered hour of anticipation.

***

Otherwise there was no lack of fine entertainment that one still remembers with gratitude: music and reading, the overture to *La muette de Portici* arranged for piano duet and played by Mother and Grandmother downstairs in the living room and delightfully interwoven with Uncle Prosper reading aloud from *Struwwelpeter* and Aunt Nanna reading from *Captain Grant's Children*. And one afternoon, Little Brother crept in with a bowl full of live baby trout that he had caught up in the river, and he lit a match in secret so that, as though in a vision, you caught sight of the tiny red-spotted fish with their transparent crystalline eyes waggling their dark fins in the clear water.

Light

Spring brought the light back. Bit by bit. The first eager sight of living reality was something you saw on the quiet by pulling the curtain aside, just a little, and only for a moment or two... but then, in a breathtaking flash, your eye has glimpsed the immense blue of the heavens, and a white cloud, and even a bird.

Then comes the blissful time when the curtain is quite legitimately drawn back, a bit extra each day, until, first wearing dark glasses and then with your naked eye, you can go out into the resurrected world, the world of daytime, of wind, of rain and sunshine, the world of the future and of eternity.

Heavy Snowfall and Compact Darkness, Indeed so Intense that from the Window in my Tower I
(Amaldus the Scribe)

can't make out a single light down in the town which I know is illuminated by a host of lamps and lights this March evening.

I have now as good as finished writing down what I had in mind on this occasion, but here I sit examining what I have written in order to see whether anything important might have been left out, and with this in mind I have brought Grandmother's old family album up here – a really impressive book, filled with a host of pictures, some fixed and some loose, most of them stuck on hard cardboard with gilt edges, as was required by the taste of that time. The binding, about which there is a scent of lavender and fulfilled destiny, is made of plush, decorated with a tarnished metal rosette and furnished with a worn and long-since slackened fastener. The many portraits accumulated here (a large number of them bearing the signature of Keil, the photographer) include almost all those who figure in this little memorial piece, but curiously enough, most of their faces look quite different in the photographs from the way in which I remember them.

For instance Father's face.

The four pictures of him all present him as a gentle, indeed almost humble man. In one of them he even has such a peaceful and indulgent expression that it actually borders on the simple. But he was tough, in many ways a ruthless loner, not only respected, but also feared by colleagues and those under his authority as well as those nearest to him, even by Mother.

Nevertheless, he was paradoxically well liked, indeed to some extent even loved by those working for him, whom he otherwise kept a tight rein on.

Father had made it the purpose of his life to re-establish the Rømer Concern, and he pursued this objective with determination and energy; in time he came to enjoy some success, although it was only partial, for the company never became the same as it had been in Great-Grandfather's day. But it was an act that gave him and others a great deal of happiness and peace of mind.

As in the case of so many other idealistic despots, Father did not primarily have his own advantage in mind. He was no self-seeking, avaricious profiteer. He was very simple and undemanding in his way of life; he rose early and usually went around dressed in an old-fashioned indestructible reefer jacket over a pale sweater, and his favourite food was boiled salted fish with potatoes and plenty of mustard. The only luxury he allowed himself were the modest rum toddies he indulged in while playing cards on a Saturday evening with loyal friends and advisers, the Numerator, the Denominator, Michelsen the bookkeeper and occasionally Debes the Lighthouse Keeper. He disliked and distrusted outer show and honours, and on two occasions he is known to have politely refused honorary consulships.

The driving force behind his firm was, however, naturally not the irresistible urge to undertake self-denying good works that naive souls often attribute to capitalists of Father's kind, but a certain determined enterprising spirit and a related indomitable imperiousness. Father was no judge of character, and his urge to dominate his surroundings could at times take on the most perverse form, as for instance in the case of Aunt Nanna, when he obstinately tried to insist on tying her to Debes, the ageing Lighthouse Keeper. He didn't succeed: the Lighthouse Keeper remained a widower, and Aunt Nanna never married. But Father's craving for power was to have fateful consequences for poor Uncle Hans, whom he imagined that stringent control could change into a good, hard-working representative of the middle-class like himself. It didn't strike him that Hans was by nature his opposite in every way: a romantic, musical young man and something of a *bel esprit,* whereas Father kept well away from both books and music. When on one occasion Uncle Hans said something about fancying going to Copenhagen to see if he could "get into acting" (an area in which he would undoubtedly have had the ability to do well!) Father's sole reaction was a great scornful guffaw and a hurtful remark to the effect that in that case he (Hans) might as well take lessons from Uncle Prosper.

The poor relationship between Father and his young brother-in-law gradually grew so bad that they were no longer on speaking terms. But one day, Uncle Hans changed tack and "gave in", as they said, and it became clear to all that the *Captain* had got what he wanted here, too, and stood as the victor.

In the constant battle between Father and Uncle Hans, Mother was mainly on her brother's side, especially with regard to one of the points of conflict, that is to say the relationship with Dolly Rose. But on this, I think I would rather quote Mother's own words in a letter to her sister in Copenhagen.

"Dear Sister,

I am writing to you with a heavy heart, the reason for which is the intolerably strained relationship between my husband and your brother. I wish you could give me some advice in my time of need. I have of course told you about the girl known as Dolly Rose, Fina the Hut's seventeen-year-old daughter who has been Hans' sweetheart and has now got into trouble. Johan absolutely *insists* that Hans must marry her, for 'a man is duty bound to take the consequences of his actions, however unpleasant they might be', and I suppose that is right enough in its way. But is it in this case? For – well, it is hard to be forced to say this, and perhaps it sounds terribly arrogant and pharisaic – but this pale little redheaded girl with the stiff doll's eyes *is* a poor retarded creature who not only cannot read and write, but who also has difficulty in expressing herself orally; indeed, she actually often reacts like a five-or-six-year-old child. She really is terribly retarded. And even if one can be furious with Hans on account of his weakness and his unforgivable aberrations, it must be obvious that it would mean nothing less than a lifelong tragedy for this still young man if for the rest of his days he was to be tied to this poor, stupid creature. Something quite different, of course, is that he can't just leave her to fend for herself, but has a duty to look after her and provide for the child. But this Johan can't see, or rather: he refuses to see it. He calls us (Hans and me) soft and cowardly and is of the opinion that Hans, 'who has drained so many pleasant cups must also drain this unpleasant one' so that he can learn some self-respect and 'grow up'.

But the worst thing is that, as things stand, he could in this way drive Hans to despair and to do himself a harm. I am sure you know what I mean, and you will hardly be surprised that I am both afraid and unhappy and pray to God that Johan will see sense after all – indeed, both Johan and Hans. But unfortunately, it does not look as though they will. Do write a few lines to me, dear Sister, and give me advice if you have any to give."

***

Dolly Rose – there is a photograph of her, too, in the old album; with her oval face and remote, faraway expression, she almost looks like some saint, and she could be called beautiful if it were not for her big, expressionless mouth with its simple, pouting lips.

After Uncle Hans had capitulated to his brother-in-law's will and married Fina the Hut's daughter, it looked as though the relationship between the two men had improved, indeed as though it was on the way to being unproblematic. Uncle Hans returned to his work in the Rømer Concern office (a job which he carried out with great talent and ease; it consisted mainly of taking care of the company's extensive correspondence with Mediterranean countries, which took almost all the fish that was exported, and with Denmark and England, whence all ordinary goods were imported.)

After the wedding, which was a quiet one, the newly-weds moved into the "Mill House", an old, impractical but reasonable house, once built by Ryberg the marketing manager and situated at the mouth of the Mill Stream in the left bay, surrounded by the old Rømer warehouses and a garden of big sycamore trees.

Virtually nothing is known of what life was like between Uncle Hans and "Aunt Rosa", except that they each had their own bedroom. Mother looked kindly after her little sister-in-law, and did her best – though seemingly in vain – to get on to some sort of terms with her. Rosa was not very good at preparing food or looking after the house, but she was both eager and capable when it came to any work in the garden. Mother got a couple of strong men to help her to get the old garden into shape after it had been a wilderness for a long time. Fina the Hut helped here, too, and rhubarb, cabbage and carrots did well in the vegetable patch, and roses, poppies and crown imperials flourished in the more decorative part of the garden, so that Aunt Rosa could set about the weeding, which after wreath-making was her favourite occupation.

Nothing ever came of the child Aunt Rosa had been expecting; the fruit of her womb left her shortly after the wedding – *if* there had ever been such a fruit, for evil tongues (and, incidentally, not only the evil ones) maintained that Dolly Rose had never been in the family way, and that it had all been scheming on the part of Fina the Hut. The slight bump that could be seen on Rosa was said to have been due to an extra heavy woollen petticoat with which her mother had equipped her. It was also thought to be quite significant that neither midwife nor doctor had been present during what was said to be Rosa's miscarriage, only Fina and one of her good friends (Spanish Rikke).

***

Uncle Hans' marriage to Rosa only lasted for just over six months. A photograph of him from this time shows a young man with a beard, expressive of resignation and self-irony, but still without any trace of the desperation to which he was soon to surrender himself, and which was to bring about a sudden end to his career.

It remains unclear whether it was a question of suicide or of some kind of desperate attempt to escape. Perhaps it was a mixture of the two. It could be established that on this unhappy boat trip, which was to be his last, Uncle Hans had taken with him a good stock of food and that he had at least a couple of thousand *kroner* in English banknotes with him when he sailed out of the bay in his big white sailing boat, the *Nitouche*, followed by a light northerly wind one beautiful midsummer morning.

It was not an unusual sight – Uncle Hans spent almost all his free time in this boat when it was sailing weather, indeed often when the sea was pretty choppy, for he had in time become a skilled shellback, whose knowledge of winds and currents even old fishermen and sea dogs acknowledged.

The *Nitouche* was an open boat, but there were some rings and staves in the stern that could hold a canvas hood to provide some shelter from rain and rough seas. Anton, the storehouse manager, who was up early and had chanced to see Uncle Hans set out, had been a little surprised that this hood was raised in spite of the good weather. He also noticed that the yachtsman set out in a southerly direction towards the open sea.

Uncle Hans never returned from this trip. A search was carried out for the missing boat for days, but in vain, and nothing is known of Uncle Hans' fate apart from the fact that one of the Rømer fishing sloops, the *Only Sister* found the *Nitouche* three weeks later drifting with its keel in the air somewhere midway between Suduroy and Shetland. There had been quite rough weather in that area during that time, a summer storm with a wind strength of ten or eleven and with heavy seas.

***

After Uncle Hans' unhappy death, Aunt Rosa stayed in the Mill House for a time together with her mother. Father later ensured that she became part of the household. In general, he took care of his brother-in-law's widow. At table, she was given a seat at his left side. He treated her with respect and attention, and she showed a child-like devotion to him to the end of his days.

***

Alas – all these *faces* that stare at me from the album's faded and mildewed columbarium. They are so reluctant to be forgotten and to vanish, and they each and every one deserved their memorial runes. But a limit must be drawn, and this is where it must be.

Finally, however – as a kind of *envoi* – a couple of words on Uncle Prosper's face!

It was fundamentally the face of a handsome man, and if you didn't know better you might well think that it was the face of a man occupied with profound philosophical thoughts on life's contrast-filled *opera semiseria*, in which we all involuntarily perform.

Uncle Prosper lived to a great age, almost ninety. He was happy to be photographed and appears sometimes in group photographs (where he is always sure to be in the foreground), and sometimes alone in "cabinet photographs", in which he looks extremely serious and confidence-inspiring, perhaps even authoritative, for Uncle Prosper had a strange ability to give the illusion of a man to whom much is entrusted and who bears a heavy responsibility.

In some of these pictures, he is wearing a silver cross on his chest; this is the decoration for meritorious services which he was awarded during a royal visit in 1907 after he had given King Frederik VIII eight very richly decorated duck eggs.

Epilogue

And now I will close the old picture book and put out the light.

The same snowfall and intense darkness.

It gives a certain feeling of light-headedness, as though you had slipped out of the context of time.

The calendar tells me that today is 29 March 1974. And yet it is something of a coincidence that this is the date and not, for instance 1874 or 1174 or merely 74 – and why not 7474 or any other date into which it might have amused the capricious forces of fate to launch a fleeting and helpless human snowflake.

There you sit, pondering in your dark tower at the end of the world and the end of life while, filled with idle speculations, you sit staring out into the silent, swarming abundance of falling snow.

***

Was there more?

There was indeed – for then you fell asleep. Aye, that was what happened to you: you slipped helplessly into a blissful sleep and the mysterious and playful dimension of dream.

What did you dream? Of course, that you were a child again. But alas – a strangely deformed and old-fashioned changeling with running eyes and melancholy wrinkles in your brows, and the bright-eyed, undaunted children you wanted to play with (so as for one last time to feel the happy young vibrancy in their life rhythm) laughed at you, not maliciously or disparagingly, just patiently. Then you, too, laughed, resigned, perhaps with just a slight touch of bitterness, while withdrawing to the dark place where you now belong, in darkness and decline beneath the merciful snowfall...

***

Was there no more then?

Indeed there was, of course. For when I awoke again after my brief snooze it had stopped snowing, and among slowly moving banks of cloud the stars were shining over the wide expanse of the sea – the beautiful crystal white of Capella, the red topaz of Aldebaran, the ecstatic group of maidens in the misty Pleiades, the flaming belt of the ever young and mirthful Orion, the whole of this enchanting heavenly springtime array. And out on the horizon there is the flashing light of the ordinary lighthouse, a mortal light among all the immortals, but in the deep, joy-intoxicated spring night nevertheless a star among other stars.